Stay away from Max Pershing or you'll be sorry

Ava gasped as she read the words. She dropped the note. Who would send such a message, and why? No one knew she'd asked Max for help, not even her mother.

Her gaze drifted to the paper again. Had Max told people he was going to help her—bragging that she'd come crawling to him for help with family business? Bile burned in the back of her throat. No, he wouldn't do that. He sincerely wanted to help her, right?

Or did he?

* * *

WITHOUT A TRACE: Will a young mother's disappearance bring a bayou town together...or tear it apart?

Books by Robin Caroll

Love Inspired Suspense

Bayou Justice
Bayou Corruption
Bayou Judgment
Bayou Paradox
Bayou Betrayal
Framed!

ROBIN CAROLL

Born and raised in Louisiana, Robin Caroll is Southern to a fault. Her passion has always been to tell stories to entertain others. When she isn't writing, Robin spends time with her husband of nineteen years, her three beautiful daughters and their four character-filled pets at home—in the South, where else? An avid reader herself, Robin loves hearing from and chatting with other readers. Although her favorite genre to read is mystery/suspense, of course, she'll read just about any good story. Except historicals! To learn more about this author of Deep South mysteries of suspense to inspire your heart, visit Robin's Web site at www.robincaroll.com.

ROBIN CAROLL

FRAMED!

Steeple
Hill®

Published by Steeple Hill Books™

Special thanks and acknowledgment to Robin Caroll
for her contribution to the Without a Trace miniseries.

STEEPLE HILL BOOKS

Steeple Hill®

Recycling programs
for this product may
not exist in your area.

ISBN-13: 978-0-373-44326-0
ISBN-10:   0-373-44326-9

FRAMED!

Copyright © 2009 by Harlequin Books S.A.

www.SteepleHill.com

Printed in U.S.A.

Trust in the Lord with all your heart,
and lean not on your own understanding.
—*Proverbs* 3:5

For Colleen Coble, who taught me so much about the craft of writing, believed I could do this, and has been a cherished friend and prayer warrior. I love and thank you, lady!

Acknowledgments

My most heartfelt gratitude to…

The other authors who worked on this series—thanks to each of you for taking the time to support and help me when needed. Your talent amazes me.

The editorial team at Steeple Hill—y'all ROCK!

Kelly Mortimer, for being my fan, my sister in Christ, my agent.

My prayer group, for lifting me before the throne daily.

My family/friends for input without measure: BB, Camy, Cheryl, Dineen, Heather, Lisa, Pammer, Ronie and Trace. I couldn't do this without you.

My family for continued encouragement: Mom, Papa, Bek, Bubba, Robert, Krys, Brandon, Rachel and all the aunts/uncles/cousins. Love you.

My daughters—Emily, Remington and Isabella—my best blessings from God. I love you so much.

All my love to my husband, Case, who was my wonderful collaborator on this story line.

All glory to my Lord and Savior, Jesus Christ.

PROLOGUE

Why couldn't she have had the foresight to ask Max to meet her in a less conspicuous place?

Ava Renault worried the necklace she wore as she stared out the front windows of Bitsy's Diner. Her mother drove her wheelchair right toward the door. If Max arrived while Charla was still there…

What was her mother doing here anyway? She normally didn't deign herself to be seen in the common diner.

Charla wasted no time rolling right to Ava's table. "Leah Farley's gone missing."

Ava covered her Mother of the Year pageant committee notes and stared at her mother. The buzz of conversation from the waitstaff in the diner must have made her hear Charla incorrectly. "What?"

"Leah Farley. You know, your brother's previous secretary. She's gone missing."

What was this? More of her mother's dramatics? Charla was nothing if not theatrical. "How, exactly, does one go missing in Loomis, Louisiana?"

"According to the news, she dropped her daughter off at her brother's house yesterday, claiming she had an appointment, and hasn't been heard from since." Charla settled her Jack

Russell terrier, Rhett, in her lap and guided her electric wheel-chair around the small dinette chair. "And just days after her husband was found dead. Isn't that curious?"

"Mother, you need to stop listening to gossip."

"That's not gossip, that's fact. It was on the local news." Charla stroked Rhett's head. "I always knew that girl was trouble. Oh, my, yes. From the first day I met her."

"Stop it. That's just being snobby."

Charla huffed. "Well, it's true. I don't know why your brother ever hired her."

Ava lifted her cup and took a sip of coffee, cooled long ago. "Maybe because she was a qualified secretary with good rec-ommendations?" She let her gaze flit around Bitsy's Diner again. Tucking the heart medallion and chain inside her blouse, she focused on her mother's wrinkle-lined face. Ava would never comment on that particular observation aloud. Charla Renault paid good money to look ten years younger than her birth certificate stated.

"Not hardly. That girl was nothing but trash."

"Enough, Mother." She set the cup on the edge of the table and lifted her pen. She didn't have time for Charla's rants right now—she needed to get her out of this diner before Max showed up and the *real* fireworks began.

But if she brushed Charla off too quickly, the antennae would come up and she'd never leave Ava alone. "Did the news give any other information?"

"Just that there are no leads, and Sheriff Reed is calling in the FBI." Charla moved her wheelchair closer to Ava and lowered her voice despite the practically empty diner. "But people are saying she may have killed her poor husband and now has run off."

"And just left her daughter here with her brother? I doubt that." Ava couldn't imagine leaving her child behind. If she had a child. She stared at her mother, the old bitterness returning. She'd once had a chance at love and happiness, a husband and children, but her mother had made sure that didn't happen.

Now she waited on that particular man to waltz into the diner and put her mother in a tizzy at seeing them together. Even if they were just working together on the Mother of the Year pageant.

Weren't they?

"I told you, the girl is trash. She'd run off and leave her child if it meant saving herself." Charla spun her chair around and rolled toward the door. Bosworth, Charla's butler and driver, opened the door, then assisted her from the wheelchair into the backseat of her waiting limo.

Ava let her mother leave without another word. What was the point? She'd learned long ago that arguing with Charla Renault was like trying to remove all the Spanish moss off the cypress trees in the bayou—useless.

Inside the diner, wait staff milled about. Dishes clanked from the kitchen. Ava stared absentmindedly out the window.

She let out a long sigh. What would make Leah Farley just up and leave Loomis? Ava snickered. Dumb question. Smart people left Loomis and never came back. Why hadn't she?

Guilt. Duty. Family. Mainly because her father had died in the same auto accident that left her mother paralyzed from the waist down. Her family had needed her then. Charla needed her for a verbal punching bag when her recovery and physical therapy frustrated her. Plus, Dylan, her brother, needed her to take care of Charla so his social calendar wouldn't be disrupted. Maybe Ava should've left when she could. But, no, she'd started her wedding planning business, I Dream of Weddings, and settled into being a business owner in Loomis, even though the majority of the weddings she planned took place in Covington or New Orleans. She continued to pray the

Lord would show her His purpose for keeping her in Loomis. So far, He'd been pretty quiet on the subject.

Ava fidgeted with her papers as Lenore Pershing, Max's mother, waltzed into the place. Ava couldn't help slouching in the chair. Again, why had she agreed to meet Max here? She absentmindedly ran her finger along her neckline, finding the necklace outlined under her shirt. She cut her gaze from Lenore and stared at the notepad in front of her. Good thing Charla had left before Lenore arrived. With the old family feud alive and well between the two families' matriarchs, that would've been a scene to end all scenes.

The notes she'd jotted didn't make sense. Her mind kept going back to Leah Farley's disappearance. On the heels of Earl's alleged suicide…Ava shivered against the ominous cold finger trailing down her spine. Was something—or someone—evil lurking in Loomis?

ONE

It was too beautiful a day to bury Dylan Renault.

Nothing but blue skies hung overhead with the sun blazing down on Loomis Cemetery. Odd for a February in south Louisiana. Where were the bolts of lightning and rolling thunder? Shouldn't the weather reflect the gloominess of the townsfolk? Not even a fog or mist to mar the beautiful Monday morning.

Ava stared at her brother's polished coffin, trying to concentrate on the Scripture being read by Reverend Harmon. She fought back the burning tears and swallowed past the lump caught in her throat.

Dylan lay in that cold, lifeless box in front of her. He would never again tug her hair or shoot her his lopsided grin. Ava's stomach roiled.

Whispers rose from the row behind her.

"Some say Earl wasn't really Sarah's father, and Dylan knew who was. And whoever he is, he's the one who shot Dylan. Probably because he knew the truth."

A different woman's voice responded. "No, I think Dylan's really that girl's father. He and Leah had a torrid love affair that went bad and she got pregnant. That's why she up and quit working for him. That's probably why she ran off three weeks ago, too."

Bile searing the back of her throat, Ava stiffened her spine and turned her head slightly to see who'd said such an outlandish thing—at the funeral of all places, too. Who'd do something so tacky?

Micheline Pershing, rumor queen of St. Tammany parish, stared back at Ava with a snooty air.

She didn't even have the decency to blush and look away when Ava stabbed her with a vicious glare. No, she met the glare head-on, even having the nerve to give Ava a curt nod in response.

Disgust inched up Ava's spine as she jerked to face the casket again and choked back more tears. Micheline was despicable. Dylan wasn't even in the ground yet, and the woman already spread lies. Not that the whole town wasn't rumbling with rumors and speculation.

Ava sighed. Who could blame them, really? Dylan had been shot in the back and left for dead in the overgrown backyard of Renault Hall, the abandoned mansion of Ava and Dylan's grandfather. Her brother's last words were what fed the gossipmongers…

"Sarah's father."

What could he mean? The only Sarah in Loomis was little Sarah Farley, daughter of the missing Leah Farley and deceased Earl Farley. What had Dylan been trying to relay? Nothing made sense, but it was hard to deny the little girl had haunting, green almond-shaped eyes, a trademark of the Renault family. Ava had racked her brain trying to figure out what her brother's dying words meant. She was as clueless as everyone else in town. The difference was she wouldn't give in to conjecture.

"Ashes to ashes, dust to dust…" Reverend Harmon's words were drowned out by Charla Renault's sobbing.

Ava patted her mother's shoulder, but her mind continued to spin. Charla had retired to her suites as soon as she'd been told about Dylan's murder, only venturing out today to attend the funeral. But to display her grief so publicly? It wasn't like Charla Renault, not at all. Hadn't she drilled into Ava over and over… *Renaults don't show emotion, Ava. We're above that.*

"Unto Him we lift Dylan…"

Ava's heart thudded at Reverend Harmon's words, recalling the last time she'd heard him utter them. Her father's funeral. The kind, loving man who'd always done what he felt was best for his family…his life taken in that horrible accident. An unfortunate accident, an untimely death that left Ava with a bitter, resentful mother to take care of. Although, Charla Renault hadn't taken long to adjust to being in a wheelchair. She'd soon been back to her usual controlling self, wreaking havoc in her children's lives.

Ava let her gaze fall on the elaborate coffin poised over the open grave in the Renault plot. Her stomach knotted as she blinked furiously.

She. Would. Not. Give. These. People. The. Satisfaction. Of. Seeing. Her. Cry.

Especially not Micheline Pershing and her cohort.

Morbid curiosity had been the only reason the good folk of Loomis had shown up at the funeral. That, or fear of disappointing Charla, who held a lot of power in the little town. They all thought Dylan had been nothing more than a spoiled playboy. They didn't know the sensitive brother she'd grown up with. The one who'd endured their mother's unfounded rages and protected Ava by sneaking them out of the house when Charla would tear into her husband. The teenager who'd kept Charla away from Ava most of her formative years.

Ava ached for his protection from the rumor mill today.

A loud moan ground out beside her. Her mother had a death grip on that poor dog, Rhett, who endured the unfamiliar hold. Charla hunched over in her wheelchair and moaned as if she'd been stabbed.

Poor choice of words. Ava licked her lips.

Again, whispers rose from the row behind her.

"Can you believe she's daring to show emotion?"

"I can't believe she even has emotions," Micheline replied. "I didn't think people with ice running through their veins had any feelings."

Ava narrowed her eyes and tossed a frown over her shoulder. The rudeness of people never ceased to amaze her. Especially here…now…barraging against her grief.

Charla let out another sob. Ava wanted to cry all the more. Never before had the matriarch of the Renault family deigned to allow anyone outside the family see even the slightest sign of weakness, perceived or real. Even when she was recovering from the auto accident, she put on a strong front, going into work everyday. Why was she giving the locals food for fodder now? Grief aside, couldn't she hear Micheline and her followers whispering about the family? Guessing about the reasons why someone would take Dylan's life?

Murdered. Ava couldn't imagine someone hating Dylan enough to kill him. Shot in the back, like some mangy cur. Sure, he'd broken a lot of hearts over the years, but she didn't think there had ever been a relationship so serious that it could've mustered enough feelings of regret or revenge to murder her brother in cold blood. As far as she knew in the business world, Dylan was a fair player. Maybe it was time she looked into the family business. Maybe Dylan had been a different kind of executive than she thought. Over the last few weeks, Dylan had changed. It seemed like he was finally growing up and becoming the man their father would've been proud of.

Even though Sheriff Bradford Reed had recently all but accused him of murdering his ex-girlfriend, Angelina Loring, who had been found dead in a swamp on the outskirts of Loomis—just after Leah Farley had gone missing.

Now Dylan had been murdered, his promising character cut down just as he was coming into his own. It was unfair, just like so many things in life. What in the world was happening to the quiet town of Loomis? Ava shuddered and shook her head.

"The peace of the Lord be with you." Reverend Harmon approached the front row and bent to take Charla's hands in his own. "God will comfort you in this time of loss."

It was as if Charla didn't even hear his words. Her tear-stained face focused on the coffin, her eyes red and glassy.

Ava swallowed, silently praying for the Holy Spirit to wrap her in peace and comfort. *Why, God? Why take Dylan from me, too? Wasn't Daddy enough?*

People stood and milled about, whispering in small groups. Screams rose in Ava, begging to be released. How could they just stand around so casually, gossiping or discussing the latest episode of their favorite sitcom? Her brother was dead…gone. He left behind a mystery no one had figured out. *Sarah's father…* Such cryptic words. It just wasn't like Dylan, so what he'd been trying to say had to be vitally important. Critically so.

Ava's friend and child psychologist, Jocelyn Gold, wrapped her in a hug. "I'm so sorry." She squeezed her before releasing her. "Are you okay?"

"I'm holding my own." Ava glanced at the tall, handsome man hovering over Jocelyn's shoulder.

Sam Pierce. FBI.

Ava let out a slow breath, struggling to recall the weeks before Dylan's murder. The FBI had been called in on Leah Farley's case and worked the attempted kidnapping, but they'd only assisted Sheriff Reed with the murder of Angelina Loring. Had Sam also believed Dylan guilty as well, or had he just been doing his job?

Sam offered his hand. "I'm truly sorry for your loss."

"Thank you." He couldn't be all bad. Not if Jocelyn was in love with him, and by all appearances, Jocelyn was starry-eyed over him. The man had a job to do and had done it, that was all. She widened her smile. "I appreciate y'all coming."

Jocelyn gave her another hug. "Call me if you need anything." She looped her arm through Sam's and headed toward the line of parked cars.

A few brave souls from her mother's generation approached Charla, offering weak sentiments of comfort. Charla accepted their gestures amid tears and clinging to her trembling dog. Ava shifted away. How sad that her mother really had no one to confide in, talk with, share her grief with. For the first time, pity for Charla rose within Ava. Her mother had no friends or confidants. Only Bosworth, the son of Charla's father's driver, who'd served Charla since she was a young woman. He'd stayed with the family through Charla's marriage, and remained her faithful servant today.

"Ava." The voice reached right into her heart and pierced it.

She spun to face Maximilion Pershing. "Max." Her gasp caught in her throat as her pulse raced.

"I'm so sorry." His eyes were the color of hot cocoa and just as soothing. He laid a steady hand on her shoulder. "I know this sounds so lame, but if there's anything I can do for you…" He paused, swallowed hard, then continued, "I hope you know I'll do whatever I can to help you."

Of all the people who offered condolences, Max meant the most to her because he knew the pain she felt. He knew her, and he understood. And maybe, just maybe, he still cared. He'd loved her once. Could he again, despite the history between them? Ava blinked back the tears threatening to spill. "Th-thank you."

He leaned closer and pulled her into his arms, hugging her gently, yet firmly.

Her heart pounded as if she'd just done twenty laps in an Olympic-size pool. Ava allowed herself to melt into his embrace. The distinct smell of his familiar cologne wafted around her. It felt so good for Max to hold her. Then again, it always had.

"I mean it. I'm here for you." His words were a caress against her ear.

For just a moment, time stood still and she was transported back to the day she'd been uprooted from her junior year of high school to go to boarding school, and she'd had to tell Max goodbye.

Wailing shattered the memory.

Ava withdrew from Max and spun around. Her mother caught sight of her. For a moment, Charla's grief disappeared, replaced with the familiar frown of disapproval. "Avvvvv-vaaaaaaaaaa!"

Only Charla Renault could make a two-syllable word draw out to ten. And in front of everyone, too.

Tossing a please-forgive-me look at Max, she mouthed "I'll call you" and rushed to her mother. Poor Rhett, the little Jack Russell terrier that never left Charla's side, quivered and whined.

She took her mother's hand and squeezed, nodding to Bosworth hovering on the edge of the crowd. Ava gave the coffin a final glance. Her stomach twisted as her heart ached to shriek louder than Charla.

Goodbye, Dylan.

She turned and guided her mother's wheelchair toward the waiting limo.

Although he hadn't known it at the time, Max Pershing had given his heart to Ava Renault years ago. Fifteen years ago, to be precise. Now he knew she still had it.

Last month, fate had thrown the two of them together again when the Loomis governing body asked him to serve on the Mother's Day pageant committee, representing the Pershing family. He'd had no choice—his mother would've been furious had he declined, so he accepted. Not knowing that his co-chair would be from the *other* prominent family in the small town—Ava Renault.

Holding her in his arms just now had confirmed it. No other woman had ever made his heart leap as Ava did.

She helped her mother into the car, gave him a final sad smile from across the cemetery, then disappeared behind the tinted glass. The Renault driver, Bosworth, shut the back door before slipping behind the steering wheel.

Every muscle in his body tensed to run after her. To hold her again. To try to smooth some of the pain etched across her face.

"Surprised to see you here." Reverend Harmon offered his hand.

Max shook hands with the man. "It's a shame what happened with Dylan. Of course, I wanted to be here for the family."

Reverend Harmon's bushy brows shot up. "The family, or Ava in particular?"

Busted. "Well, it's no secret there's no love lost between my mother and Charla, that's for sure."

"But between you and Ava?"

Reverend Harmon knew their history—knew how they'd been falling in love back in high school, knew how Charla Renault had been unable to accept such an idea and had sent Ava away to boarding school, knew how Charla had brought Ava back to attend the local university when she'd learned Max had been accepted at Louisiana State University. Everyone who knew the story seemed as bewildered as Max over why, when he returned from college, Ava had avoided Max like the plague. Too much parental influence, or had her feelings toward Max changed?

"That's ancient history."

One of the cemetery workers approached. "Reverend Harmon, most everyone has left. Is it okay to lower the casket now?"

The man's demeanor changed in an instant. "Of course." He nodded to Max. "I'm praying for you."

How was he supposed to respond to that? He didn't want anyone to pray for him. He'd learned years ago that God wasn't listening. He hadn't listened to Max's pleas to bring Ava home and then had turned a deaf ear to Max's requests to save his cousin, Michael Pershing, from pancreatic cancer at such a young age. But Max couldn't fault Harmon for his faith. Everyone knew Reverend Harmon was a good man, had a good heart.

Max stood silently as the reverend said a final prayer over the casket containing Dylan Renault, then the casket was lowered into the grave. Max's gut knotted.

People weren't supposed to die so young. And murdered! In Loomis. The third one in a month. Plus, Leah Farley was still missing, although the general consensus was that she was dead as well.

The town fed on gossip and suppositions. FBI agents and investigators had barraged Loomis and set up base in the downtown area. Just two weeks ago, they'd focused on Dylan Renault as a suspect in Angelina Loring's death. Now he'd been shot and killed. What was the city coming to?

Max headed to his truck, his steps dragging as much as his heart. With everything going on, all the deaths and Dylan Renault's cryptic dying words, the town hummed with rumors of what was happening. The fact that his and Ava's mothers continued to feud just added to all the tension.

And Ava Renault sat right in the dead center of it all.

He parked outside his condo, the property his mother owned. At least her condo was across the complex from his. He had to agree with Charla Renault on one thing—his mother had made the complex quite a sight with its baby blue paint and gaudy design. He still couldn't figure out if his mother really had such bad taste or if she'd done it on purpose just to annoy Charla. Their generations-old feud, fueled by competitive business deals and now the lonely older women with nothing to do but stir up trouble, was never-ending.

Max unlocked the door, tossed his keys onto the buffet in the entry and headed to the kitchen.

"How was the funeral?"

Max startled and then faced his mother. "Why are you here?"

She sat at the dinette table, sipping tea as if she belonged. But she didn't. This was *his* home, not hers. Yet she'd never seemed to have gotten the message. "I wanted to know how the funeral went."

He opened the fridge and poured a glass of orange juice. "You don't care. You hate Charla Renault."

"Well, of course I do. But that doesn't mean I don't want to know who all turned out for the funeral. Anything interesting happen?"

"Mom, I can't believe you'd stoop so low. I'm not going to gossip about the funeral." He shook his head.

"Don't make it sound like I'm some horrible person. Charla Renault would be just as curious if it were your funeral." She sniffed and stood, taking her teacup to the sink and rinsing it out. "I wonder what the police are thinking now since Dylan was their prime suspect in that poor Angelina's death." She tsked.

Max slugged down the rest of the orange juice. "That's not a very nice attitude, and you know it."

"But it's the truth." She lifted her purse, sarcasm dripping in her words. "I've seen you with that Ava Renault several times in the last month or so. I recognize the look she's giving you. She's trying to get her claws into you again."

"We're working together on the Mother of the Year pageant committee, that's all."

Her eyes narrowed for a moment. "Awfully defensive, aren't you? Maybe you know I'm right."

Nope, she was wrong. Ava couldn't get her *claws* into him again…she'd never retracted them.

TWO

Yesterday left scars upon her soul.

Ava hadn't had such a horrible day since her father died. Not only had she buried her brother, her only sibling, but she'd also been hugged by Max Pershing. Not just physically, but a soul hug. Talk about scars.

Initially, she'd been appalled to find he was her co-chair for the Mother of the Year pageant committee. On uneasy footing, they'd awkwardly stumbled through a couple of weeks of working together. Then, as if the planets were all in alignment, they'd fallen into a comfortable pattern of being together.

It felt an awful lot like old times.

Now, her heart fluttered just thinking about being in his arms again. Had she made a mistake in honoring her mother's demands for so long? Could Max still have feelings for her, or was she merely misinterpreting his kind condolences yesterday?

"Ms. Ava, Bosworth says Sheriff Reed is here to see Ms. Charla, but she refuses to open her door when I knock." The maid hovered in the doorway to the dining hall, literally wringing her hands.

Ava stood. "Don't worry, Bea. I'll let the sheriff know Mother isn't feeling well." She smoothed down her suit pants.

"Tell Bosworth to show him into the library and let him know I'll be along shortly."

"Would you like me to serve coffee?"

"Please." Ava smiled as the woman left, then sucked in air. What could the sheriff want? Did they have a lead on Dylan's killer? Or was he here to try even harder to link Dylan to Angelina Loring's death? Since her brother was dead, how could they? She straightened her shoulders and headed to the library.

St. Tammany parish's sheriff, Bradford Reed, stood with his back to the door, facing the marble fireplace. He touched the gold frame on the mantel holding Dylan's picture. She recalled the manner in which he had focused on Dylan in regards to Angelina's death. He'd been so wrong. She knew that in her heart. Resentment clawed at her chest. She said a quiet prayer, hoping to grasp a measure of peace.

Ava said "amen" and entered the room. "Sheriff Reed, how may I help you?"

He faced her, a stoic look pasted onto his aging features. "Ava." His gaze ambled over her shoulder. "Where's Charla?"

"Mother isn't feeling well today, Sheriff." She gestured toward the sofa. "Would you care to have a seat?"

Dropping to the sofa, he nodded as she sat in the high-back chair diagonal from him. "Well, I appreciate you seeing me."

After the way he'd treated her brother, she had to stretch to put on politeness. "But of course." She picked imaginary lint from her pants as she fought to remain poised, the urge to ask why he was here nearly suffocating her. But she wouldn't. It wasn't deemed proper hostess behavior.

"I'd like to ask you a couple of questions about your brother, if I may."

"Certainly." More questions, but no answers. After burying Dylan yesterday, she'd hoped for at least *some* promising news.

"Good." Sheriff Reed pulled out a notebook and pencil. "First, what can you tell me about the relationship your brother had with Angelina Loring?"

So much for hoping. Ava shifted in her seat. "Didn't you cover all of this when you centered your attention on him as a suspect in her death?"

A little tic by his eye was the only visible reaction. "We just have to check every angle, every clue."

"Then, as I told you before, they went out socially together some, but it wasn't a serious relationship by any means." She paused, recalling how Angelina seemed to cling to Dylan as hard as she could. "Well, it might've been for Angelina, but Dylan never got serious in any relationship." Ava tilted her head. "Do y'all now think the murders are related?" Were they finally realizing Dylan had nothing to do with Angelina's death? His death had to have them scrambling for answers. Unraveling their loosely knit theory.

Dylan was dead. Correction, murdered.

"We're just looking at any and all possible connections."

"But she was found dead in the swamp, and Dylan was shot in the back. Do you think they're related?"

Sheriff Reed fingered the edge of his notebook with calloused hands.

"Angelina was shot in the back, too, wasn't she?" She refused to give in to the urge to glare at him. No wonder they'd searched the mansion when they'd convinced themselves Dylan had killed Angelina. But they would've never found a gun—there wasn't a firearm in the house. Not since her father had died and all his hunting shotguns had been destroyed.

"We didn't make the details of her death public for investigative reasons."

Because they had suspected Dylan. "But was she shot in the back just like my brother?"

"Ma'am, can you think of any reason someone would want your brother and Angelina dead?"

Answering a question with another a question confirmed it—Dylan and Angelina were both shot in the back. Evil *had* arrived in Loomis. "My brother, no. And trust me, I've thought of every possible scenario. A lot of people didn't like Dylan, but I can't think of anyone who hated him enough to kill him."

"Maybe a bad business deal?"

"I wouldn't know. I'm not exactly in the family business. But neither Dylan nor Mother mentioned anything serious going on at the company." The thought struck her again that it was high time she did know what went on behind closed doors at the Renault Corporation.

"Would they have?"

"Of course." Ava paused as Bea entered the library with a silver service that she set on the iron-and-glass coffee table.

After the maid had poured and been dismissed, Ava settled her cup in its saucer and stared at the sheriff. "You know my mother's ruthless reputation…she isn't any different at home. If there'd been a business transaction that hadn't gone well, she'd delight in calling Dylan on the carpet every opportunity she could. We all shared dinner every night, except when I had a wedding or Dylan had a date." Because Ava sure hadn't had a meaningful date in longer than she could remember.

Max's image floated across her mind.

"I see. Was that often? That Dylan had a date, I mean?"

Ava shook her head, banishing Max from her thoughts. "An occasional date during the week and most weekends. Is this really necessary?"

"The more we know, the better we can work the case."

Because now they were looking for a link between the murders. Perfectly logical, but the loss was still too new for the memories not to hurt. Ava took a sip of her coffee and waited.

The sheriff took a noisy sip from his own cup. The china rattled as he replaced it on the saucer. "There aren't many young, single women in Loomis your brother didn't date. And some who weren't single."

Ava folded her hands in her lap. "Not that I see any relevance in this discussion, but Dylan enjoyed being around women. He liked women, pretty much all women. I didn't know that was illegal, or a reason to be a murder suspect."

"I mean no disrespect, you understand, but I have to do my job. I have others breathing down my neck …"

"Like the FBI?" No disrespect? He sure wasn't singing that tune when they'd questioned Dylan relentlessly after Angelina's body had been found floating in the bayou close to Renault Hall. "I understand, Sheriff, I do, but if you're trying to link Dylan's dating a lot and not being serious about any one woman to a reason he would murder or be murdered, I believe you're looking in the wrong direction."

"Where should I be looking, Ms. Renault?"

"I haven't a clue. I'm not in law enforcement, Sheriff Reed." She hated the snippiness that had crept into her tone but couldn't help it. The whole discussion bothered her, rubbing her fresh wounds raw.

He cleared his throat. "What about Angelina Loring?"

"I didn't know her well enough to give supposition."

"But your brother dated her, off and on, for some time."

Great. Make her feel more like a heel of a sister. "I didn't invest a lot of time in anyone Dylan dated. If he got serious, he would've told me and I'd have taken the time to get to know the person."

"I see." No, he didn't, but what more could she say?

"What about him dating someone else with red hair? Aside from Angelina?"

"I wasn't Dylan's social secretary."

"Can you think of anyone he mentioned going out with who had red hair?"

Why was he hung up on red hair? "Sheriff Reed, is there something I should know?"

He reviewed his notes, refusing to look at her. "We found a long, red hair on your brother's clothes and are trying to see how it could have logically gotten there."

That was new. "I haven't a clue."

He nodded. "I know the FBI already asked you about Leah Farley."

She shifted, crossing her legs at the ankles. "Yes. Do you think there might be a connection there? That hardly seems likely. Leah hadn't worked for my brother in more than three years."

"But evidence now suggests there might be a link between your brother and Mrs. Farley."

"Because of his last words, right?"

"Yes. Do you have any idea what they could mean?"

"As I told you before, Sheriff, I have no idea what Dylan was trying to relay with his final words. No idea whatsoever." She only wished she had an answer.

"But Mrs. Farley most likely wouldn't have liked whatever explanation there is for his words, don't you think?"

"I couldn't say." Wait a minute. Were they now going back to the theory that Leah had killed Earl, Angelina, and now Dylan? Actually…now that she thought about it, Leah did have a connection to all three of them. A very strong connection.

"I see." He stood, pocketing his notebook. "So you wouldn't have any personal knowledge about Mrs. Farley looking into real estate prior to her disappearance?"

"Just what I've heard about town." Now where was he going?

"Or anything about a connection between Earl Farley and Georgia Duffy?"

"No." Grasping at straws, that's what he was doing. Although, rumor had it that Georgia and Leah's husband, Earl, might've had something interesting going on. Still, Ava knew firsthand how rumors were often untrue.

"Heard anything about Mrs. Farley firing Ms. Duffy as her real estate agent?"

"Sure, the town was talking about it, but I don't believe gossip, Sheriff."

He let out a harrumph. "I think those are all my questions for now." He passed her his business card. "If you think of anything else, even if it merely strikes you as odd, call me. A deputy will be by to deliver Dylan's personal effects that we've released. We're still going through some effects taken from his office."

His personal effects. How impersonally stated.

Ava stood and accepted his card. "Bea will see you out."

As if on cue, the maid appeared in the doorway. The sheriff paused at the door and glanced back at Ava. "I'm sorry for your loss."

She just bet he was. "Thank you."

Alone again, Ava plopped into a chair. Her thoughts drifted to her last conversations with her brother. Dylan had told Ava that he'd broken off things with Angelina because she'd started to get too serious, talking about love and future. To her brother, such discussions were the kiss of death in a relationship.

A long, red hair? Maybe they were still reaching to link him to Angelina's death. But she'd been found six days before Dylan was shot. It didn't make any sense.

Nothing made sense except her grief.

Maybe the sheriff had stumbled onto something about it being work related. Maybe it was something Dylan was involved with that he kept hidden from Charla. Ava could certainly understand—their mother hunted for reasons to interfere in their lives. But Ava had no way of knowing what Dylan had been working on. Ava stiffened her spine—all that would change now.

Her mother had pushed Ava into following a *female* career. How many times had Charla lectured that a man of stature, one Ava was expected to find and marry, wouldn't be interested in a domineering businesswoman? Ava laughed at the irony. Charla Renault had always been a shrewd businesswoman, taking over her father's business when he died. Marriage hadn't stopped her, didn't even slow her down when she had children. As a matter of fact, she'd never even taken her husband's name when she married. Nor did she give her husband's last name to her children.

"May I take the tray, Ms. Ava?"

She nodded at Bea, determination settling into her chest. Charla was in no condition to oversee anything, much less the multi-million-dollar corporation bearing the family name. All the hard work and time Dylan had invested in the company shouldn't just go down the tubes. The time had come for Ava to take the bull by the horns, as her father would've said. Ava stood and crossed the hall to the study. Hovering over the desk, she made her decision and called her assistant at I Dream of Weddings. Cathy would have to take over the planning for the Halloway wedding in New Orleans next week, because she would make sure the Renault Corporation continued to be successful.

After instructing Cathy to not book anything in the immediate future that she, herself, couldn't oversee, Ava pressed the speed dial number for the Renault Corporation.

It was time to take control, to become the businesswoman she knew she could be. One who could run a corporation as intelligently as Charla Renault, but with a heart—and a soul.

Now was Ava's time.

* * *

The last vestige of the sun's rays streaked across the February sky. Max smiled, loving this time of the year, driving home from work when the day had already given way to welcoming the night.

It'd been a long day. Busy, but productive. There were so many calls today from locals wanting to invest in real estate that if Max didn't know better, he'd think people needed tax write-offs. But it was the wrong time of year and he did know better—the influx of people with money to spend was directly due to Dylan Renault's death. People were nervous over the leader of Renault Corporation being dead, and from what Max had witnessed at the funeral, it didn't appear Charla Renault was in any condition to take over the helm of the investment corporation.

Max didn't like what'd happened, yet he wasn't stupid. His own business would suffer if he didn't provide the service his company was founded upon. But he didn't have to like making a profit off Ava's loss.

Speaking of Ava, she hadn't called like she said she would. He tried not to be disappointed, tried to rationalize that she probably had a million things to do, but his heart sank to his toes. Max entered his home, his mouth watering for the stir-fry he planned to make. He'd been so busy he'd only had time to gulp down a sandwich from the vendor who made daily visits to the offices along Main and Church streets. His stomach rumbled at the memory.

"Working late?"

Max glared at his mother. "What are you doing here again? You can't just keep letting yourself in, Mom. This is my home."

"I just miss you is all." She used the tone of hers that bordered on whining. How often she'd lamented the fact he'd moved into his own condo years ago.

Did she really think he'd just live with her forever?

"Look, I've had a long day at work, and all I want to do is make a little stir-fry, catch the news and call it an early night."

His mother smiled. "Can I join you? I'll help cut the vegetables."

He opened his mouth to protest, then stopped. His mother didn't have many friends, mainly because she'd spent her life dedicated to him. While he'd never asked her to, she'd sacrificed everything to see to his happiness. Max let out a sigh. "Sure. Grab the squash and zucchini from the fridge and start chopping."

He'd just set up the wok when the phone rang. "Hello."

"Max?" Just the way Ava said his name made his stomach quiver, and it wasn't from hunger.

"Ava. Is anything wrong?" His mother's hand froze, knife poised over the squash. She arched a well-drawn eyebrow. Max moved into the living room.

"No. Yes." Ava hesitated. "I don't know. Sheriff Reed was here, asking questions. He's got me all confused."

"How so?"

"Trying to make a connection between Dylan and Angelina Loring and Leah Farley. All these deaths."

"I thought the police had wrapped them all up. Well, except for Dylan's."

"They liked Dylan for Angelina's murder, but now…well, they found a long, red hair on Dylan's clothes, and I don't think it was Angelina's. Not by the questions the sheriff asked. And I'm still trying to figure out why Dylan was even at Renault Hall." She sighed. "It doesn't make sense."

"Maybe he went by just to check out the property. Maybe he was considering getting the area appraised." He tightened his hold on the phone.

Ava snorted. "Not hardly. Mother forbade us to even step foot on the property."

"You never know. Things change. So do people."

"I suppose."

He hated hearing the pain in her voice. It did strange things to his gut. "Do you want me to come get you and take you somewhere?"

"No, I just wanted to vent a little." Her voice hitched as she drew in a shaky breath.

She didn't have anyone to talk to—certainly not her mother, by the way she'd carried on at the funeral.

"We can go somewhere and talk." He ached to hold her again. Smooth her silky hair and tell her everything would be okay. "I meant what I said. If there's anything I can do for you …"

"I appreciate that, but maybe I should just call it a night."

"You can call me anytime, you know."

"Thanks, Max." The smile came through in her voice.

"Good night, Ava." Turning around to head into the kitchen, he nearly ran smack into his mother hovering in the hallway.

"You're going to see her? Ava Renault?"

He nudged past her and set the phone on its base. "No, I just made the offer."

"Why?" His mother cut the knife through the air. "She's not good enough for you, never was. She's nothing but trouble."

After setting the temperature on the wok, he sliced a chicken breast. "Mom, she's not trouble. She's grieving, for pity's sake."

Lenore pointed the tip of the knife at his face. "You mark my words, Maximilion, if you get tangled up with her again, she's gonna break your heart. For a second time."

He didn't bother answering, just reached for the bell peppers.

And hoped his mother was dead wrong.

THREE

Sleep had remained as elusive to Ava as the mystery surrounding her brother's death.

Now, determination to prove herself in the corporate world drove her to dress in a classy business suit and head downstairs.

Rhett's barking beckoned Ava down the hall to her mother's suites at eight. As per usual these days, the door was shut. Ava rapped softly. "Mother?"

"Go away and leave me alone."

The temptation to flee nearly spun Ava in the opposite direction, but she couldn't disregard her mother's grief. Squaring her shoulders, Ava turned the knob and pushed open the door. The little dog met her, prancing and whining. "Have you let Rhett out this morning?"

"I told you to leave me alone." Charla sat in her wheelchair facing the window, her back to the door.

Ava ignored her mother's bitter tone and crossed to the patio door, then flung it open. Crisp, early February air swirled through the rooms. The little dog burst outside into the yard. She faced her mother and nearly gasped aloud. Never before had she seen her so…so unkempt. No makeup, her hair in total disarray, and in the same outfit she'd worn to the funeral. Had she slept in those clothes?

"Will you please leave now?"

Maybe she should. She certainly didn't know what to say. Every instinct she had urged her to do as her mother requested, but her heart wouldn't allow her to budge.

Ava cracked the patio door open wider, allowing the air admittance. Once the stuffiness had been banished down the corridor, Ava faced Charla, hands on her hips. "Mother, I know you're grieving—I am, too. Please don't shut me out. I miss Dylan terribly." Tears clogged her throat.

"Don't talk to me about missing him." Charla's voice raised an octave and quivered. "He always was too weak for this earth. Letting himself get distracted and led astray. Just too much like his father…"

Ava swallowed as disappointment crawled up her spine. "I know you're crushed, but don't push me away." She softened her tone. "We're it, Mother. All that's left of the family. We should be pulling together, not mourning alone."

Charla's bright green eyes, identical to Ava's, filled with moisture. For a moment, Ava detected a softness in her mother she'd never seen before. A vulnerability of sorts. A blink later, it was gone. "I'd like you to leave now."

Ava teared up as well, despite trying not to break down. "Mother, please don't do this. We need each other." She all but begged.

Before Charla could speak, the little terrier bolted back into the room, so full of vigor his little body quivered.

Ava stared at her mother, her emotions knotting. She'd never been able to run to Charla for comfort, even as a child. Her father had been the one who held her when she had nightmares, kissed her bumps and bruises, put ointment on her scraped knees. Her mother had never shown any maternal instinct. Now that Ava thought about it, Charla hadn't ever shown any affection for her daughter. Sure, she'd doted on Dylan, but never Ava.

Bitterness held Ava's tongue. Charla called Rhett into her lap, gripped him tightly and glared. "Just leave me alone."

She clenched and unclenched her hands at her sides, fighting for what composure she could retain. "What about the Renault Corporation, Mother? Are you going to ignore it as well? The company Dylan put so much time and energy into?"

"I can't even face the office—reminders of my sweet boy are everywhere." Charla narrowed her eyes.

That answered that. There was no reasoning with her, and Ava didn't have the strength left to argue. Or to ask for control of the company…yet.

She shut the patio door and marched from the suites without another word. After turning the corner of the hall, Ava pressed her back against the wall. She closed her eyes and slid to the floor.

Daddy…Dylan…no one to turn to now. *Dear Lord, please give me strength and peace.*

The pent-up tears spewed from her eyes, making warm tracks down her cheeks. She didn't care. Let them fall where they would, Ava couldn't hold back the pain any longer. She'd never felt so alone in her life. At least after the car accident, Dylan had been there to hold her and soothe the loss of their father. Drawing her knees to her chest, she rested her forearms atop her knees, then laid her head on her arms, sobbing without control.

Max's image flitted across her mind. She didn't have to be alone if she didn't want to be. He said he'd be there for her.

Ava shook her head and wiped her face against her sleeve. Now she was being downright silly. After the way she'd brushed Max off the last several years, it was a miracle he even spoke to her, much less be willing to help her in any way.

"Ms. Ava, are you okay?"

Ava pushed to her feet and swiped her sleeve over her eyes

again. "I'm fine, Bea." She smoothed her shirt. "Was there something you needed?"

The elderly lady cocked her head. "Just checking on Ms. Charla this morning." Concern etched into the lines deep in her face.

The woman had been with the family since Ava was a toddler. If anyone knew Charla Renault at all, it was Bea. Or Bosworth, who had been with Charla even longer. Since childhood, really.

"Mother's still not feeling well."

"Oh."

"Thank you, though." Ava held her head high and strode to the office. Only when she was ensconced safely behind the massive oak doors did she collapse in the kid leather chair, her eyes again spilling with tears.

She glanced at the picture on the corner of the desk. Her father and Dylan had their arms over each other's shoulders, their silly, smiling faces posing for Ava behind the lens. Tears flowed from her eyes. Why both of them?

Sniffing, Ava cleared her throat, but questions still niggled against her mind. What about the red hair found? What had Dylan been doing at the abandoned Renault Hall? He had to be meeting someone. That was the only logical explanation.

Meeting his own murderer.

Just the thought sent shivers down her back. She needed to do something. To talk to someone.

Max.

Amazing how her fingers pressed the numbers of his cell so quickly, as if they moved of their own accord. She gripped the phone tightly. What was she doing calling Max at this hour of the morning? She shouldn't bother him.

"Hello." His voice was a nice mix of baritone with Southern drawl.

"Hi, Max."

"Ava. How are you?"

"Holding on. I'm going to head into Renault Corporation and see where the business is. Try to make heads or tails of everything."

"I'll be more than happy to help you catch up, I mean, if you'd like input from someone with an MBA."

"As opposed to someone who is just-a-nothing wedding planner?"

He hesitated. "I didn't mean any offense, Ava. Just offering to help."

"I know. It's just that very reaction is what I ran into when I called the office. The office manager seemed shocked I even knew where the building was located." She twisted the phone cord around her finger.

"I'm at your service, ma'am."

She laughed, throaty and humorless. "Well, I'm smart enough to know I'm going to need help, and I don't believe the workers will think I'm worthy to be brought up to speed." She paused, her breathing a bit erratic over the thought of working with him, side by side. "I gratefully take you up on your offer. Can you meet me at the office at ten?"

"I'd be honored. But, uh, Ava, you realize your mother will have a fit if I so much as park in the parking lot at Renault Corporation, right?"

"You saw her at the funeral. There's no way she can oversee the company right now."

"You'll need to get your company lawyer to obtain a power of attorney over the corporation—otherwise, you can't sign anything."

Something else she'd have to handle. Alone. "I'll get on that."

"What about your business?"

"My assistant is handling things for the time being."

"Then I'll see you soon."

"I really appreciate it." Her words lilted with relief. "I mean it, Max. I really do appreciate your willingness to help me out."

"No problem."

The familiar beep of another call coming through sounded against her ear. "We can talk more when I see you."

"Looking forward to it."

She pressed the button on the phone to answer the other call. "Hello."

"Ava? It's Jocelyn."

"Hey, girl."

"How are you?"

"I'm fine. As well as can be expected." Ava traced the engraved scrollwork on the edge of the desk with her fingernail.

"If you want to talk, you know I'm here for you."

Ava smiled, knowing her friend actually meant what she offered. "I know. I'm holding my own." She glanced at her appointment book. "About to dive into work. It'll at least keep my mind occupied."

"That's actually one of the reasons I was calling."

"Really?"

"Sam and I are getting married, and we'd like you to plan the blessed event."

"Congratulations." Ava glanced at her planner again. "When were you thinking of having the wedding?"

"As soon as you can plan it, if you feel up to it."

As if she wouldn't plan her close friend's wedding? Then again, Sam had questioned Dylan. She tried to remember… Dylan being a suspect in Angelina's murder had been Sheriff Reed's idea. Wait a minute—Jocelyn said as soon as possible? "Um, is there any particular reason for the urgency?"

Jocelyn laughed. "Just that we've wasted enough time, don't you think?"

Ava chuckled as well. Joceyln's excitement was contagious. "Of course. I'd be happy to plan your wedding." When she'd have time, she hadn't a clue. "When would you like to meet to set a date and go over preliminary details?"

"Sam and I are both free tomorrow morning. How about the breakfast buffet at the hotel? I'm actually thinking that might work for the wedding reception."

Nodding, Ava grabbed a pen. "Let's plan on, say, nine tomorrow morning?"

"Perfect. Thanks, Ava."

The morning sun shone down on Loomis, despite the fogginess hovering over the bayou. Max slipped his sunglasses into the truck's holder after parking at Pershing Land Developing. He gazed next door at their real estate office. At least Georgia Duffy's car wasn't in the lot. He'd dodged the bullet again. Ever since he'd broken up with her years ago, the woman seemed determined to worm her way back into his life. She'd even gone so far as to work at Pershing Real Estate. The fact that she lived in Pershing Plaza didn't help matters, either.

He headed into the building on Church Street, nodding at the receptionist on his way to his office.

"Why, Max, aren't you here bright and early?" Patsy Thomas, his secretary, sounded shocked.

He smiled as he unlocked his office door. "Good morning to you, Patsy." He winked and turned on his lights. Since he normally came in around ten, he understood her surprise at his darkening the door before nine. "I'm just getting work lined up for the troops as I'll be out of the office most of today."

Helping Ava. Getting to be with her again. Working with her.

Patsy followed him into his office, taking his jacket to hang on the brass hooks behind the door. "Playing hooky, are ya?"

"Sort of." And with the only person he wanted to play hooky with. "Will you bring me the February projections report?"

"Certainly. I'll bring it with your coffee."

Max grinned at the secretary who'd served him for more than five years. Patsy was about twenty years older than he and almost motherly, but not in the same manner as Max's own mother. No, Patsy couldn't compare with Lenore Pershing. Patsy was kind and gentle. Not a control freak. "Thanks."

Once alone, he booted up his computer and checked his e-mail. The flood of business had his agents booked solid for the rest of the week. Fear of what would happen to the Renault Corporation after Dylan's death had everyone running for cover. Ava truly did need his help.

Charla Renault, now there was a woman who could give his own mother a run for her money in the control-freak department. That they were arch rivals and had been for decades… well, it just fit. Everyone in Loomis had long ago picked which side of the feud they fell on, and were very careful not to stray too close to the middle… All because of a marriage that went bad and a public embarrassment generations ago. It made no sense to Max. Then again, there'd been a couple of business deals that went sour because of the family feud over the past couple of years. Still, that hadn't been enough to send Ava away to boarding school…had it?

Patsy tapped on his door and entered without a response. She set a steaming cup of coffee on the desk in front of him alongside a spreadsheet. "Anything else?"

He took a sip of the black coffee. Strong, just the way he liked it. "Thanks, Pats. I really appreciate it."

"Want to tell me what's going on?" She perched on the arm of the leather chair facing his desk.

"I'm just helping out a friend. She needs help managing her company on a temporary basis." He took another sip, then stared at his secretary.

"What friend?"

He shrugged, but felt the heat creeping across his face. "Just a friend from school who needs a bit of advice."

Patsy stood and made a clucking sound with her tongue. "That friend wouldn't happen to be Ms. Ava Renault, now would it?"

Max grinned. "Does it make a difference?"

His secretary chuckled, loud and hearty. "Not to me, but I bet it does to your momma. What's Lenore say about this?"

The smile slid off his face. "She's none too happy."

"Bet that's putting it mildly."

"Yeah." He ran a finger around the lip of the cup. "But I just have to help Ava out." He lifted his gaze to his secretary's face.

"I understand." Patsy moved toward the door. "Have a good day, and I'll hold down the fort here."

"Thanks, Pats."

Someday, sooner rather than later, he was going to have to sit his mother down and tell Lenore to back off from his life. Once he figured out what he really felt for Ava, he would.

Confusion wreaked havoc in his heart. Ava definitely sent him mixed signals—ignoring him for years, even going so far as to cross the street to not have to pass him, refusing any eye contact with him, then working with him on the committee and allowing him to hold her at the funeral. Okay, so she'd been grief stricken. But now she'd called. Twice. Surely that meant something.

Meant she needed help.

No, Ava wasn't a user. Not like her mother. Or like her brother had been.

Max cringed. He hated to think ill of the dead, but truthfully, everyone in Loomis knew Dylan was a heartbreaker. He used women's feelings for him when it suited him. And many times, it suited him. Although a couple of weeks ago, he seemed to have changed.

He'd have to think of a way to tell Ava what he knew without setting off her alarms. He'd started to when she asked questions on the phone, but she'd dismissed him. Maybe he'd get a chance today when he worked with her. The idea of working with her lifted his spirits, he had to admit.

Patsy rushed into his office and shut the door. "Max, the sheriff and a deputy are here to see you."

His heart sank as he struggled to stand. "See me? Whatever for?"

"They said they had some questions for you. Both of them."

In a bigger city, two local lawmen showing up wouldn't be a big deal. But here, in St. Tammany parish, if more than one in uniform came with questions, it had to be bad news. Very bad.

Max swallowed against a dry mouth and nodded at his secretary. "Show them in, please, Pats."

FOUR

Talk about an icy reception—the abominable snowman would shiver.

Ava stared at the office manager blocking the doorway to Dylan's office. The older woman managed to emit disdain from every pore of her self-righteous being. "I don't know that the sheriff has completed his search of Mr. Renault's office. No one's been allowed in since...since Mr. Renault passed."

Passed? Dylan was murdered. "The sheriff's finished in here, I assure you." Ava took a step to move around the woman, but Mildred Fontenot wouldn't be deterred.

She shifted in the doorway. "Mrs. Renault never allows anyone to enter her or Mr. Renault's private offices."

Enough! That fine line holding together the last of Ava's resolve snapped. She propped her hands on her hips. "I'm sorry, but do you see the last name on the outside of this building? It's Renault, *my* last name. This is *my* family's business, and I'm going into *my* brother's office to work. Period. Now, please, step aside." She'd get that power of attorney pronto.

Mildred hesitated.

Ava continued to stare in the manner her mother had demanded she perfect years ago. The one that could be considered haughty. With a slight tilt of the head, a jutting out of the chin, it dared anyone to defy.

The office manager stepped out of Ava's way, but her expression screamed she didn't like it one little bit.

"Thank you." Ava stepped across the threshold and shut the office door soundly. Score one for everyone who refuses to be intimidated.

Celebration over her victory was short-lived. The smell in the office engulfed her, cocooning her in the scent of her brother. His cologne, the hint of his shampoo…her senses assaulted, Ava wobbled to the couch and collapsed. Even the constant hum from his empty fish tank accosted her memories. How many times had she made fun of him for having a huge aquarium with no fish? He just liked the calming sound. Or he had liked it.

What she wouldn't give to obtain some calmness right now.

Ava exhaled slowly and got to her feet. She trembled as she made her way to the large mahogany desk. Dylan's desk. She sank into the leather chair and let her gaze wander over the stacks of papers and folders. Ashamed to admit it, Ava didn't know if this was Dylan's working style or not. How long had it been since she'd even stopped by the offices? Why hadn't she made it a point to meet her brother for lunch at least weekly? So many wasted opportunities. Maybe if she'd spent more time with him, she'd have a clue what his dying words meant.

She shook her head and swallowed the tears threatening to erupt. Better stiffen her spine before Mildred stormed in and tried to kick her out. With a sigh, she flipped open the first file she came to and peered at the documents inside.

It was all Greek to her. She didn't even understand the spreadsheet of investments. This was going to be harder than she imagined. Thank goodness Max had volunteered to come and help her. Until then, she'd just do a little search of Dylan's desk. Sure, the sheriff had looked around, but how hard was he *really* investigating? He was so close to retiring and didn't have the experience for so many back-to-back murders. He'd been sure Dylan was involved in Angelina's death. How would he know if he stumbled across something important? He wouldn't. Not that she would, but she had to try. Maybe she'd notice something out of place or odd.

She'd start with the right top drawer, where even in his office at home, Dylan kept his appointment book and personal items. He'd had carpal tunnel surgery on his left hand a couple of years ago, and ever since, he'd instinctively put everything on the right side.

The drawer was empty. Nothing but a few rubber bands and paper clips scattered against the wood. Not even a pencil. Ava let her hand rest on the handle. Of course, law enforcement would've taken any and everything deemed possible evidence. At least they were working the case. Well, truth be told, probably the FBI investigators. Sheriff Reed was only going through the motions.

After slamming the drawer shut, Ava checked the other drawers but found them as empty as the first. Frustrated, she turned her attention back to the files. She might not know what all the papers inside meant, but she could look over the names. She knew these people, knew some of their secrets. Maybe Dylan had been murdered because of a business deal gone bad, like Sheriff Reed had suggested. She still couldn't fathom how the business could be connected to Leah and Earl Farley, and Angelina, but who knew? It was no more outlandish of a theory than Dylan murdering Angelina.

As she stared at the files, it occurred to her that if there was motive for murder, it wouldn't be sitting on the desk, out in the open.

Think, Ava, think.

Her fingers automatically reached for the medallion hanging from a gold chain around her neck, a habit she'd had for a decade. Touching the heart, her thoughts went to Max. With clarity she recalled the day she'd given him the matching necklace. The summer before her senior year in high school. They'd been sweethearts, until her mother had found out and blew a gasket. Charla had her first "episode" right after it became public that Max and Ava were an item. She put her foot down, despite Ava's father's appeals. No child of Charla's would ever be involved with a child of Lenore Pershing. Ever. Two days later, Charla had the arrangements made…Ava would complete her senior year at a boarding school in New Orleans. The night before Ava left, she snuck out of the Renault Mansion—the first time ever—and met Max at the abandoned Renault Hall.

Moon shining brightly, Ava waited under the cypress tree covered in Spanish moss. The musky scent of the bayou drifted on the warm August air. Max stepped from the shadows, his arms open to her.

She moved into his embrace, reveling in the comfort and security he provided. Tears wet her cheeks as she lifted her face for his kiss. Their stolen moment passed much too quickly.

"I'll wait for you to come home." His voice came out shaky, unsteady.

"I love you."

"I'll love you always."

Reaching into her pocket, she pulled out a velvet box and handed it to him. His eyes glistened as he took two chains from the case. From each one dangled a medallion engraved with one of their names around a stemmed rose, full of thorns. He put the one with Ava's name around his neck, swearing to cherish it until they could be together again. She did the same with his.

"Even apart, we'll always be together." He lowered his head to hers again.

The opening lines of "Louisiana Saturday Night" rang out from her cell phone, startling Ava back to the present. She jumped to her feet and rushed to the couch, grabbed her phone from her purse and flipped it open. "Hello."

"Ms. Renault?"

Not many people called her Ms. Renault. "Yes?"

"This is Patsy Thomas. Max's secretary."

A vise caught around Ava's heart. "Yes?" The word came out in a breath.

"Max asked me to let you know he'll be unable to come to your office this morning."

"Oh." Disappointment slammed against her chest.

"An unavoidable emergency came up that he has to handle, but he asks that you meet him at Vincetta's Italian Restaurant at noon."

What to say? Having his secretary call her—what did that mean?

"He said to tell you if he could've postponed this issue, he would have, but he'll explain over lunch if you'll let him."

She swallowed hard. He'd given her the benefit of the doubt about why she hadn't come rushing back into his arms, and their relationship, when he'd returned to Loomis. He had even offered to help her with the business. Now the tables were turned.

"Sure. I'll meet him there at noon."

"I'll make the reservations now." His secretary's voice sounded pleased.

Had he conveyed to his secretary that meeting with Ava was important?

Seriously?

Max had to shake his head, mentally only, of course. The sheriff thought meeting with Dylan the week before the murder gave him, Max, motive?

"I've told you, I met Dylan at the property only to give him my professional assessment of the land's value."

"Why wouldn't he have met with one of the real estate agents, not you? It's no secret you guys weren't friends. Why would he have sought you, of all people, out?" Sheriff Reed sat on the edge of Max's desk, grating on Max's nerves.

"Maybe because he didn't want anyone to know yet."

"And why's that?"

"I don't know. He didn't say. He just asked me to keep our meeting quiet."

"Hmm." Sheriff Reed pushed to his feet while Deputy Olson scribbled in a notebook. "Gotta admit, Max, it sounds fishy, don't it?"

Truth was, it *did* sound fishy. Max still wasn't totally sure why Dylan had called him and asked to meet him at the abandoned Renault Hall. Max had been shocked to hear Dylan claim he wanted to get a rough estimate on the property itself—being so close to the swamp and all. If he built a house, would the value be increased or should he think of building elsewhere? Max had been skeptical, but Dylan had seemed sincere, truly interested, ready to break away from Charla's controlling issues and build a place of his own.

Now, telling everything to the sheriff, he had to admit it sounded lame.

It would to Ava, too.

Why had he ever agreed to meet Dylan? Why hadn't he handed the meeting off to one of his agents, or better yet, recommended a good appraiser?

Because he thought helping Dylan might earn him a spot in Ava's good graces. After all, they'd been working on the committee together for a couple of weeks, finding a connection with one another again in some small way.

But Dylan had asked Max not to mention his idea to anyone,

not even if he was asked. Not even if Ava was the one asking. A hard request to honor, but Max had.

Until now.

"Seems kinda odd that Dylan would request you keep it a secret, yet list your name and the meeting place and time in his appointment book."

"I can't explain that." The sheriff was right—Dylan's actions did seem contradictory to his words.

"Uh-huh." The sheriff nodded at Olson, who put away the notebook. "Guess I don't need to tell ya not to leave Loomis. I'm sure the FBI will want to talk to you."

Max nodded and stood. "Like I'd skip out of town?" He let out a dry laugh. "I have nothing to hide."

"Right." Sheriff Reed followed his deputy out of Max's office, leaving Max to his own thoughts.

How was he going to explain this to Ava? He'd have to do it before she heard it through the grapevine, which Loomis was incredibly famous for. Just when they'd gotten their relationship on an even keel, now this. Would she listen to his explanation? Understand?

"Are you okay?" Patsy stuck her head in the office door.

"Yeah." Max let out a sigh and ran a hand over his hair. "Just frustrated."

"No explanation needed." She smiled and winked. "But you'd better hurry so you don't miss your lunch date with Ava. I took the liberty of making y'all reservations at Vincetta's."

"But how…?"

Patsy's smile widened. "I took it upon myself to tell her you'd explain missing y'all's meeting by making it up to her at lunch. She's meeting you there at noon."

He bent and hugged his secretary. "I think it's time I put in a raise for you."

"Past due." She chuckled and gave his arm a playful slap.

"Now, get before you're late. Mustn't stand a lady up twice in one day—women don't like that. Especially women like Ava Renault."

Max grabbed his jacket and headed out the door to keep his date.

One turn and two blocks later, he whipped into the parking lot of the restaurant. He needed to tell Ava about meeting Dylan. No use in procrastinating. If he'd learned anything about Ava Renault, it was that you couldn't plan a conversation with her. She was a surprise. Just like the night she'd snuck out of her house to tell him goodbye. He'd been about to suggest they elope, when she gave him a medallion with her name engraved on it. A medallion just like the one she had with his name on it.

He snapped his keys into his pocket and stepped from the truck. He needed to remember to get the necklace to the jeweler. A month ago, he'd broken the chain while playing racquetball at Clancy's Gym. As he'd driven his car that day, he'd put the broken necklace into his car's console. That he needed to get it fixed totally slipped his mind until this moment. It was the longest he'd gone without wearing it under his shirts since the night they parted. He made a mental note to get it out of the car tomorrow.

The restaurant hostess greeted him at the door and led him to a corner table where Ava sat perusing a menu.

She was as breathtaking today as she'd been fifteen years ago. Blond hair with the slightest hint of auburn mixed in, especially when the light hit it just right. Almond-shaped eyes in a haunting shade of green that was nearly impossible to describe. She caught sight of him and smiled.

His heart stuttered as he took the seat across the table from her. "I'm so sorry about this morning."

The waiter appeared, cutting off any remark she was about to make. After taking their drink orders of sweet tea, the waiter launched into the lunch specials of spaghetti and lasagna, then rushed away.

"I hope everything's okay." It was a statement, but the way she said it made it sound like a question.

A pregnant pause filled the air. Tension hovered like the mist over the bayou in the early morning hours. Here it was, his prime opportunity to tell her, to explain. He took a deep breath, sucking in the strain, and gripped the linen napkin in his lap.

The waiter reappeared with their drinks. "Have you decided what you'll be having?"

Ava ordered the Italian salad, while Max said he'd try the lasagna special. The waiter retrieved their menus and left.

"So…" Ava lifted her tea and took a sip.

"Sheriff Reed came by to ask me a couple of questions."

She sat the glass back to the table with a clunk. "About?"

"I had a meeting with your brother the week before he was killed." Max held his breath and studied her face for her reaction.

He wasn't disappointed. Her beautiful eyes widened and her mouth formed an O. "You met with Dylan? Why?"

Here it was—the moment of truth. He let out his breath. "He called and asked to meet with me."

"Whatever about?"

He swallowed against a dry mouth. "About the property Renault Hall sits on."

She blinked slowly…once, twice, then pressed her lips together until they formed a straight line. A long moment passed before she spoke in a hushed tone. "What about it?"

"He wanted my opinion on what the property was worth."

She arched a single, dainty eyebrow. "Really?"

Max nodded and let the words trip over themselves as he

explained. When he was done, Ava said nothing, just kept staring at him with those hypnotic eyes. Her expression never wavered, not one iota.

"He never said a word to me about this. I can't imagine what he was thinking." Wasn't that an understatement? Mother would've had a fit if she even suspected Dylan was interested in that land. Period. Maybe he wanted to sell the land because of its close proximity to where Angelina had been found? No, Charla wouldn't hear of such. What could he have been thinking?

From what she could tell from the company's accounting— as near as she could figure from her examination this morning—the Renault Cooperation had a very prosperous cash flow. Nothing made sense. She peered across the table. "Did he tell you why he was interested in the land's value?"

Max lifted a casual shoulder. "He wanted to know an approximation of what I thought the land was worth. He wanted to know if I believed the value would increase if he built a house there, after tearing down the old estate."

Now *that* was ludicrous. Charla would never allow a house, any house, to be built upon the property, and Dylan knew that as well as she.

"He didn't want anyone to know what he was considering."

It hurt that her brother hadn't trusted her with this information, that he had instead turned to someone he'd considered an enemy. Both Dylan and Max had been raised to be competitors, and they'd complied as they grew. Little League, high school football, and now as adults, business competitors. Yet he'd trusted Max over her? Why? Something didn't sound right.

"I don't know why he was interested."

The waiter delivered their meals and a basket of hot bread.

The mouthwatering aroma of Italian spices wafted over their table, but Ava couldn't even look at her salad. And then a shocking final realization stole her appetite.

Max had met with Dylan a week before he'd been shot—at the murder scene.

FIVE

Morning dawned bright and sunny despite Ava's dark mood. Why couldn't it be a typical February day, dismal and gloomy? At least her breakfast with Jocelyn and Sam had been pleasant. Sam had been especially cordial. The image of him with Jocelyn didn't match the tough-guy image of him as an FBI agent. Maybe he had to be that way at work. But now she had a million things to do to get their wedding planned by the end of the month. So much to do, not enough time.

The shocker to her morning had come when she slipped behind the wheel of her car. Clint Herald and his niece, Sarah Farley, walked along the sidewalk. Ava's heart caught. *Could* the rumors be true? Surely her brother would have said something if Sarah had been his daughter, right? Sarah had blond hair that shone in the morning sun.

Turn around and let me get a good look at your eyes!

But Clint led the little girl into one of the shops. The question burned in Ava's mind the entire drive home.

"Ms. Ava, Bosworth says a deputy's here with a box of stuff that was Dylan's. Mrs. Charla won't answer her door." Bea's voice broke into Ava's mental wanderings. The maid stood in the doorway of Ava's suites, the morning sun filtering in from the open drapes and bathing her in a warm glow.

Ava stared at the maid through the mirror. She'd just changed into a business suit to go into the Renault Corporation. Now this. *Lord, I need a little help down here. I'm running on empty in the strength department.*

"I'll be right down. Just take the deputy to the sitting room, please. I'll see to Mother after I've dealt with him." Ava waited until the maid had left to grip the edge of her vanity so hard she nearly broke a carefully manicured nail.

The situation wasn't getting any easier as time went on. First her mother's odd behavior, then the questions by Sheriff Reed, then finding out about Max and Dylan's meeting and now having to go through her brother's belongings. And all the questions, too. *When will it ease up, Lord?*

After Max had delivered his news over lunch yesterday, he'd returned to Renault Cooperation with her and spent the afternoon explaining the spreadsheets as well as the profit-and-loss statements for each client's investments. His assistance had been more than valuable, and despite the questions warring in her mind about the strange meeting between him and Dylan, she'd greatly appreciated his help. It was still very odd for them to have met only a week before the murder, and at the crime scene, too, but her heart wouldn't believe that Max had anything to do with Dylan's murder. It was all circumstantial, and Max had explained what happened.

Even if it didn't make sense. No wonder the sheriff had questioned him.

Dylan had been questioned several times about his connection with Angelina. The investigation had to be worked. But Max couldn't be involved. He just couldn't be.

Ava had been up most of the night, tossing and turning the facts over in her mind. Nothing was what it seemed. She didn't have time to ponder it yet again—there was a deputy with her brother's belongings waiting for her downstairs.

Dread dragged her steps as she made her way down the elaborate staircase, her fingers grazing the polished-to-a-shine cedar rail. She'd have to check on her mother after she finished with the deputy. It just wasn't healthy for Charla to lock herself in her suites. Not at all. Maybe she should call Jocelyn to come by and try to talk to Charla. She couldn't go on like this— something had to give.

She stiffened her spine as she entered the sitting room. Deputy Aaron Bertrand stood in full uniform and lifted a cardboard box as she walked into the room. "Ms. Ava." He dipped his head in lieu of being able to tip his hat to her.

"Deputy." She stopped at the settee table and gestured toward the box. "Are those my brother's things?"

"Yes, ma'am. Is Ms. Charla coming?"

"No. Mother still isn't feeling very well. I'll handle this."

He set the box on the table, then withdrew a piece of paper. "I'll need you to sign the inventory sheet after you've gone through everything. Just to make sure what we logged is all there."

Which meant she had to go through Dylan's stuff now, with Deputy Bertrand watching. So much for grieving in private.

She pushed down the lump rising up in her throat and nodded. With shaking hands, she opened the flaps. She took a deep breath and stared at her brother's belongings.

How strange to see a dead person's things. Disturbing and depressing. Especially things that belonged to her brother. Her gut twisted.

The lawman cleared his throat. She wanted to scream that this was very hard, and not to rush her, but knew this was only a job to him. He probably had places he needed to be, crimes to investigate.

She withdrew Dylan's money clip, the platinum holder with his initials monogrammed on the outside. The metal was cold to her touch, but she remembered the warmth in Dylan's hug when he thanked her for it at Christmas. Had it only been two months ago? Only his driver's license, credit cards and cash were wrapped tightly inside. She glanced at Deputy Bertrand. "Obviously, this rules out robbery as motive for his murder."

"Yes, ma'am."

She set the money clip on the table and pulled out a watch. A Presidential Rolex with a diamond bezel—a gift from Charla on Dylan's birthday two years ago. Ava set it beside the money clip. "Definitely not robbery."

The deputy didn't comment, just shifted his weight from one leg to the other, silently urging her to get through the box.

Ava withdrew a plastic bag filled with coins and other items and shot an inquiring gaze to Bertrand.

"Those effects were on his person at the time of his death."

"Where in particular?"

"In his pockets. His clothes are in evidence and won't be returned."

"Oh." As if she'd ever want to see the clothes her brother died in. Creepy. Turning her attention back to the bag, she couldn't tell what was inside because everything jumbled together. She dumped the contents on the table.

Loose change, a monogrammed golf ball marker, and…her heart caught.

A medallion with a rose and engraving.

Her insides trembled as much as her hands as she picked up the piece of jewelry. She ran her thumb over the engraving. Her name. Max had kept it all these years?

No, it couldn't be.

"We think he probably got it as a surprise for you or something, although it wasn't in a jeweler's box," the deputy said. "It's a little dirty because we dusted it for prints. Not a useful one in the bunch. Just smudges."

Fingerprints? Who cared about fingerprints? How Dylan got this was the question. And why Max kept it for so many years. Her fingers went automatically to her matching necklace. She yanked her hand down quickly, hoping the deputy didn't notice. "This was in Dylan's pocket?"

"Yes, ma'am."

"Are you positive?" Her mouth was drier than Loomis in August.

He glanced at the inventory sheet he held and nodded. "It lists it right here: coins and ball marker found in right front pants pocket, medallion found in left front pants pocket."

"But that can't be." *Dear Lord, this can't be happening.*

"Why's that?"

"Dylan shouldn't have had this at all. I gave this to Max Pershing back in high school."

Another day, another opportunity to see Ava.

Max wasn't surprised that he started his day thinking of her. Just being in close contact with her for the past month or so, he'd already gotten accustomed to spending time with her again. Old habits die hard. Or was there a chance for a reunion between them?

For the last several days, his feelings toward Ava had resurfaced with a vengeance. His heart tripped every time he saw her, yet his mind needed answers. An explanation as to why she avoided him when she returned to town. Answers to why she'd never made contact with him in college, never even replying to his letters. They'd been in love—what happened to change her feelings? Had she gotten involved with someone else in college, while he was in Baton Rouge? He found that hard to believe as the rumor mill kept everyone up to date as to the relationship status of everyone in Loomis. So, what'd happened?

Not knowing the truth set his teeth on edge. He could not allow himself to fall head over heels again until he knew.

With that thought, Max grabbed his keys from the buffet and headed out of his condo. Birds chirped happily in the Bradford pear trees lining the walkway to the parking lot. By all appearances, it would be an early spring.

"Why weren't you in the office yesterday?"

Max nearly tripped at the sound of his mother's voice. She stood by his truck, hand on hip. "I called more than five times. That secretary of yours is useless."

"Good morning, Mom." He planted a peck on her upturned cheek, grateful that she'd reminded him to put in for Patsy's raise. "I had things to attend to."

"What kinds of things? And why couldn't your secretary tell me? I'm your mother."

A detail she never let him forget. He let out a sigh. "If you must know, the sheriff had some questions for me."

Her eyes widened. "What questions?"

She'd hear soon enough. Actually, he was slightly surprised she didn't already know. Was his cousin Micheline slipping? "About my meeting with Dylan Renault the week before his murder."

Shock didn't look nearly as good on Lenore as it did on Ava. Max filled her in on the details and waited for the outburst.

One, two, three, fo—

"What? They implied you could be involved with his murder? How dare Bradford! I was a major contributor to his re-election campaign. He and I…well, I can't believe this."

Max rested a hand on her shoulder. "It's okay. Really. It may sound bad, but that's okay. I have nothing to hide. I told them the truth and that should be the end of it."

"But to accuse you…"

"They didn't accuse me. Just asked me questions."

"Still." His mother continued to fume, her lips pursed tightly.

"It's all fine. Don't worry." He pressed a kiss to her forehead before opening his truck door. "I'm heading into the office now."

"What does Ava think?" Her words stopped him.

"What?"

"Ava. What does she think about your connection to her brother's murder?"

How *did* she feel? She'd been bewildered by her brother's motivation, but other than that, she really hadn't said much. Maybe he should've pressed her to talk more yesterday.

"I can't imagine she'd want anything to do with you anymore after finding this out."

He focused on his mother's face. Her eyes. "I really don't think that's any of your business." His words were sharper than he'd intended, but, honestly, how could she derive pleasure from his situation?

Her expression changed. Went slack. "I'm sorry, I didn't mean to offend you. It's just that the Renaults are so shallow, so concerned with their appearance that I thought she'd brush you off just on the implication. I don't want you to be hurt, honey. I only care about you."

He sighed and softened his tone. "I know, but truly, I'm okay. Ava and I are doing some things together. That's all."

Max didn't miss her huff under her breath. "I'm a big boy, Mom. Able to take care of myself."

"Does that include your heart, too?"

He smiled and slipped behind the wheel of his truck. If only he knew the answer to her question. His office was only a block away, so he didn't have time to question the issue long. Max went directly into the personnel office and put in a healthy raise for Patsy before going to his own office.

Sinking into his plush executive chair, he dove into the work piled on his desk from his absence yesterday. Amazing how much could stack up from just an afternoon away. He was a third through the heap when Patsy stuck her head in the doorway. "Boss, Sheriff Reed's here to see you. Again." She wrinkled her nose.

His heart thumped hard against his ribs. "Send him in."

Sheriff Bradford Reed ambled into the office, his gait as worn and tired as the man himself.

Max stood and shut the office door. "What can I help you with today, Sheriff?"

"I'm gonna need you to come down to the station for questioning."

What? Max's pulse raced. "Whatever for? I answered all your questions yesterday, did I not?"

"New evidence has surfaced that puts you at the scene of Dylan Renault's murder."

No way. The old man must be mistaken. "What kind of evidence?"

"We'll discuss that at the station."

"Are you arresting me, Bradford?"

"Not yet." The sheriff finally made eye contact with Max. "Either you can come with me now or I can get a warrant and have you picked up and brought in. I thought it'd be easier for you this way."

Warrant? Hauled into the station? This was serious—more than a sheriff rushing through evidence. "Should I call my lawyer?"

"That's up to you."

Just as he'd told his mother hours ago, he had nothing to hide. The truth would clear him of any implication. He'd told the sheriff everything he knew. Maybe this was just a scare tactic. Didn't law enforcement play mind games to catch their man? Only problem was, they were way off base if they thought he was involved.

"So, which way is it gonna be?"

"I'll follow you out." Max opened the door and waved the sheriff through. He gave a brief nod to Patsy as he passed her desk. Her eyes were wide with concern. He gave her a quick wink.

Once in the parking lot, Max stepped toward the crosswalk.

"I'll need you to ride with me."

Max paused. The sheriff's station was just across the street. Why on earth had Reed driven over? Maybe he *should* call his lawyer.

The sheriff waited, holding open the back door to the cruiser.

Nah. He'd be fine. He had nothing to hide. Max slipped into the backseat and nearly gagged. The air reeked of stale cigarette smoke and alcohol. Had Chuck Peters been picked up and hauled into a cell to sleep one off again? It sure smelled like it.

Sheriff Reed put the car in gear and sputtered across Church Street, then eased into the parking lot. He took his time opening the back door with the protected locks.

Max pulled his long frame out of the car, grateful he hadn't had to ride far. His legs would've cramped in such tight quarters. He glanced around, taking note of the townsfolk rushing about on their lunch hour. Great. Within an hour, both Ava and his mother would have heard about his trip to the sheriff's station.

The only question was…would Max be coming back out?

SIX

How would Charla react?

Ava paused outside her mother's door, wondering if she should bother to say anything. Charla had never found out about the necklaces, but now that Ava'd given a statement identifying it as the one she'd given to Max years ago, it wouldn't be long before Charla knew everything.

Yet, with the way she'd secluded herself lately, Charla wouldn't have opportunity to hear all the gossip. A silver lining, perhaps?

Rhett barked at the door. Ava rapped softly on the wood. "Mother?"

"Just leave me alone."

Ava let out a sigh. Same old, same old. It was getting tiring mighty quick. While wanting to turn and leave, she fingered the papers the lawyer had brought with him after the deputy had left. She had to get these signed. The lawyer, Paul Fayard, sighed behind her. Slowly, she gripped the door and inched it open. "Mother?"

"I said, leave me alone."

Shock rocked Ava to the core. Her mother sat in her wheel-chair, still wearing her bed jacket. Turning to the lawyer, she motioned for him to wait.

"You're a mess." Ava crossed the floor, slapped the papers onto the writing table and twisted open the blinds. Sunlight streamed into the room.

Charla squinted and held her hand up to block the light. "Stop that!"

"No, I won't." Moving to stand before her mother, Ava fisted a hand on her hip. "I know you're mourning Dylan. I am, too, but you've got to start taking care of yourself. When was the last time you had a shower? Yesterday? Day before?"

Her mother turned her head, avoiding Ava's stare. "I don't want your help."

"Then maybe I should call Jocelyn."

Charla's glare could melt the moss off a cypress tree. "I don't need to talk to anyone. Especially not a *child* shrink."

"You need to talk to someone." Ava lowered her voice as she moved a step closer to her mother's wheelchair. "You aren't dealing with your grief in a healthy manner." She waved at the tray on the ottoman. "You haven't even eaten the lunch Bea brought in. You're losing weight. Do you want to just waste away?"

"Is there a healthy way to deal with the loss of my only son?" Moisture made Charla's eyes brighter. "I'm dealing in my own way, which I'll continue to do." She sniffed. "Now, what do you want?"

That sounded more like the old Charla. Maybe she *would* work through her grief on her own.

Ava retrieved the papers from the desk and handed them to her mother. "Until you're ready to return to the office, someone needs to oversee the Renault Cooperation. I'd prefer it be a Renault."

Charla chuckled, the sound devoid of humor. "You? Are you suggesting I allow *you* to manage the company?"

Ava bristled, praying the lawyer on the other side of the door didn't hear Charla's snide comments. "I do run my own business, Mother."

"A wedding planning business. Not exactly a Fortune 500 company."

"Which you encouraged me to become. Still, I know basic business accounting. I spent yesterday going over the files on Dylan's desk and was able to understand his system." Thanks to Max, but she wouldn't go into that little detail just yet.

"So you want to try your hand at running my company?"

"Unless you intend to start going back to work immediately, yes."

Charla's brows formed a crooked line over her cold, emotionless eyes. The Renault green eyes. "Fine."

"Our lawyer's waiting outside to notarize your signature."

"Paul? Well, don't leave him out in the hall. Bring him in." In a flash, a glimmer of the old Charla Renault came through. She smoothed down her silver hair and gestured for a pen. Ava retrieved one quickly and passed it to her mother before opening the door.

Paul Fayard stepped into the room, not bothering to hide his surprise. "Mrs. Renault." He stood off to the side of the wheelchair as if leery of getting too close.

"Here, I'm signing." Charla scrawled her name across the bottom line, then handed the papers to the lawyer, but glared at Ava. "Don't mess up my company."

Ava didn't bother to reply, just stood as Mr. Fayard signed the papers under Charla's handwriting and affixed his seal.

Her mother stared at her for a long moment before waving them away. "Let me be now. You've worn me out. I need to rest." Again, her demeanor changed in an instant.

Ava left her mother's suites and headed toward the front door, struggling with emotions that left her raw. "Thank you for coming on such short notice, Mr. Fayard. I really appreciate it."

"Is she going to be all right?" The lawyer who'd been representing the Renaults for nearly a decade wore his age in the lines around his eyes.

"She'll be fine. We're adjusting to Dylan's death."

"And I'm sure not having his murder solved isn't helping." He slipped the papers into his designer briefcase. "I'm sure this is difficult for you as well. With Dylan having been a suspect in Angelina's death, and her working for you."

"It's tragic about Ms. Loring. I feel for her mother. But I don't get emotionally involved with any of my clients, or my employees."

"I understand." But his words had been just a tad too snippy for her not to think there might be more than he was saying. Her throat tightened. "The sheriff is working the case."

Paul Fayard threw back his bald head and laughed. "Bradford? He's on the fast track to retirement and getting a cheap gold watch." He sobered. "Is the FBI helping in the investigation?"

Ava shrugged. "From what I understand, they are."

"Then maybe you'll get some answers."

"I hope so."

"I heard through my legal connections that the FBI has determined the hairs found on Earl Farley and Dylan's bodies came from a wig. Natural hair, but from a wig."

Ava stiffened at the announcement. Why hadn't she been told this? "So, the other murders *aren't* solved? They may truly be connected to Dylan's murder?"

"From what I hear, anything's game. And they believe Leah Farley could very well be dead."

"But they haven't found a body."

He shook his head. "Honey, there's a million places in the swamp to hide a body that nobody will ever find." He shrugged. "But I hear forensics should be concluded on her car very soon."

"I thought it was burned so badly no evidence could be recovered."

"You'd be amazed at what modern technology can do these days."

Ava squared her shoulders, reeling from the revelations learned. "Well, again, thank you for coming by." She extended her hand. After they shook, Bosworth appeared at Mr. Fayard's elbow.

"If you need anything, you know how to reach me."

She nodded, her hand automatically reaching for her necklace, only to remember Deputy Bertrand had taken hers for evidence along with the one she'd given Max.

The one found in Dylan's pocket when he'd been murdered.

She shuddered at the thought as she passed through the garage and slipped into her car.

Her heart warred with her head as she drove down Main Street. Just when the old feelings she had for Max were brought front and center, all this happened. What was she supposed to think, to feel?

Stopping at the light on the corner of Main and Church, she glanced at Pershing Real Estate. Georgia Duffy, standing by her red convertible, waggled her fingers in a wave. Ava gave a curt nod, then drove another block.

Something about Georgia rubbed her the wrong way. Maybe it was the fact that Georgia had dated Max after he returned from college. She knew because even though she'd avoided the gossip and going out in public places where she could see Max on a date, her mother had taken great delight in rubbing their relationship in Ava's face.

Wait, Georgia had red hair. If Dylan had been seeing her, that would explain why Ava didn't know. Dylan would never have told her, knowing how just the mention of Georgia's name set Ava's teeth on edge.

Maybe her aversion to the woman was silly. But Georgia, even in high school, had gone out of her way to flaunt her good looks around. She'd been the popular girl in school, the one everyone liked, while so many had avoided Ava because of her mother. Ava had always felt like the ugly duckling around her, so when she'd heard about Max dating her, Ava had seen red.

She parked her car and strode through the glass doors of Renault Cooperation. The receptionist smiled as Ava waltzed by. Ava jabbed the up button in the elevator and tapped the toe of her shoe as the car rose.

Once inside Dylan's office, she shut the door, grateful she hadn't run into Mildred this afternoon. But what to do? She didn't want to be here without Max—didn't even know where to begin, but she also didn't want to go home and face the tomb of a home Renault Mansion had become. If only she could determine what she wanted.

Max. Her heart's instinctive response jolted her.

With everything pointing to him as a suspect…could she continue to think he couldn't be involved? Her heart so wanted to believe that the young man she'd fallen in love with could never be involved in her brother's murder. Yet logic screamed to look at the evidence. A secret meeting at the crime scene the week before the murder, a flimsy excuse, at best, for the reason of the meeting, Max's medallion in Dylan's pocket…what all did it mean?

Lord, I can't believe Max would have anything to do with Dylan's murder. I pray You'll send me wisdom and guidance.

Mildred opened the door to Dylan's office, files in hand. She stopped short when she spied Ava. "Oh. I didn't know you were here." Her expression clearly showed her disappointment.

"I am and will be. Mother gave me control over the Renault

Cooperation this morning." She shouldn't have enjoyed the widening of Mildred's eyes, but she couldn't help herself. "In the future, please knock before you enter *my* office."

A cotton field took up residence in his mouth.

Max stared at the medallion in the plastic bag Sheriff Reed waved in front of his face. "Don't bother to deny it's yours—Ava Renault already identified it as the one she gave you." He lifted another bag that held Ava's necklace, hers still on its chain. "Matches hers."

Ava already knew. She'd identified it. What could she be thinking right now? "Yes, it's mine."

"Care to explain how it was found in Dylan Renault's pocket when we arrived at the scene?"

What? "Excuse me?" Sweat lined Max's palms.

"Your medallion was found in Dylan's pants pocket. How do you suppose it got there?" Sheriff Reed tossed the bags onto the table.

The cramped interrogation room grew still and close. Heat crept up the back of Max's neck. "I have no idea."

"Really?" The sheriff turned to his deputy and tossed a snide look. "You confess it's yours, but you have no idea how it came to be in Dylan's possession? Guess you think it's just some strange coincidence?"

This was going from bad to worse. "Look, the last time I saw the medallion was when I put it into my car's console the day I broke the chain."

"How'd you break the chain?" Deputy Bertrand interrupted.

"Playing racquetball."

"When?" Sheriff Reed jumped right back in.

"Uh, I'm not sure. A month ago maybe."

"Where?"

Max shifted against the hard wooden chair. The questions came fast and furious. "Clancy's Gym."

"Who were you playing with?" The sheriff and deputy tag teamed him. Both lawmen bore down on him, leaning over the table.

"I—I can't remember right now." Who *had* he been playing with?

The sheriff straightened and crossed his arms over his chest. "Special Agent Sam Pierce from the FBI would like to talk to you."

The FBI? This *was* serious. "Should I call my attorney?"

The door opened and the FBI agent sauntered into the room. "Do you need a lawyer?" The man's dark look and stature commanded attention. Not to mention his accent—not Louisiana or Cajun, very out of place.

"I'm innocent, if that's what you're asking." Max struggled not to fidget.

Sam paced in front of the table. Max had seen him around town, talking to people about Leah Farley and her disappearance. He'd also been called to the scene of Angelina Loring's death. But all those had been solved, or so they'd thought for a while. Until Dylan had been shot. Now it seemed everything was opened wide again. Well, except for the attempted kidnappings.

"You know, Max, I'm not from here. I don't know all the dynamics of this feud your family has with the Renaults, but I know y'all don't like each other." Sam ran a hand through his hair. "So I have to ask myself, with such a long-standing dislike of one another, why would Dylan Renault ask for a meeting with you about anything? And how did a medallion of yours end up in his pants pocket?"

Max swallowed against the aridness of his tongue. They were going to build a case against him and charge *him* with Dylan's murder!

"We'd like you to give us a sample of DNA and your fingerprints," Sheriff Reed said.

Sam darted a glance at the aging sheriff.

DNA and fingerprints? Oh, yeah, they were going to charge him with this crime. Max gritted his teeth. "I'd like my lawyer now."

The FBI agent let out a heavy sigh and nodded to the sheriff. "Get him a phone."

Sheriff Reed ambled out the door, his deputy on his heels.

Alone in the room with Sam, Max struggled to breathe normally while his heart raced. They were probably watching him through that double-sided mirror. He was innocent—he had nothing to hide, but this G-man acted like he'd found a smoking gun in Max's hand.

"I'm telling the truth."

"Do you know how many times I've heard that over the years in my career?" Sam leaned against the cinder block wall. "Want to guess how many times it was a lie?"

Max clamped his lips together. He shouldn't say another word until his lawyer got here. Thank goodness Pershing Land Developing kept an attorney on retainer. Sure, he was a real estate lawyer, but he worked for a law firm that surely had someone with experience in situations such as this.

A criminal situation. Murder. The implications raced around Max's brain.

"Know what I think?"

Max raised his gaze to Sam's face and lifted his eyebrows. The smooth FBI agent wouldn't get him to say a thing without a lawyer present.

Sam kicked off from the wall and towered over the table. "I think you did meet Dylan at Renault Hall the week before he was killed, and I don't think it had anything to do with the land value. I think it had to do with his sister, Ava."

Max sucked in air.

"I think Dylan heard the rumors floating around town about you and her working together on that pageant committee. I think he got worried his sister was going to get involved with you again, and he wanted to stop it. I think that's what the meeting was about."

Max fought not to react or respond.

"Gossip says too many people saw you together, looking rather cozy. Bet that just burned Dylan up. So, what, did he meet with you and ask you to stop seeing his sister? Was that it?"

Clenching and unclenching his fists under the table, Max didn't flinch. This guy had it all wrong.

"Did you say no? Get in each other's face?" Sam scrutinized Max's expression. "I think you did. I think that meeting ended badly."

Max worked to control his breathing.

"I think you called him the day of the murder and told him you'd reconsidered. Asked to meet him again, same place."

Oh, this wasn't looking good at all.

Sam straightened and gestured in the air. "Don't worry—we're already working on getting a warrant for your phone records. Home, cell, office. It's only a matter of time."

Which would disprove this arrogant agent's theory.

"And Dylan did meet you, didn't he? He did, thinking you were going to agree to leave his sister alone. Only he got a bigger surprise. Maybe he saw that medallion and realized you'd pulled one over on him. Maybe you taunted him with it, telling him you could see his sister and there wasn't a thing he could do about it."

Talk about barking up the wrong tree. This guy wasn't even in the right park.

"What happened then? Exchange of punches? You know,

the autopsy report reflected a couple of bruises in the abdominal area that weren't explained. Did he rip the chain off your neck? Go to slip it in his pocket and the chain fell off?"

Max's heart pounded. This guy really thought he'd murdered Dylan. Over Ava.

"He got the best of you, so you got the gun you probably brought with the intention of shooting him and shot him in the back. Then you grabbed the necklace off the ground and ran, not realizing the medallion had made it into Dylan's pocket. You left him for dead. Is that what happened?"

Biting his tongue to keep from screaming out how absurd the idea was, Max tightened his jaw.

"I think that's exactly what happened. And you watch, we'll prove it. We're getting search warrants for your home and office and autos as we speak. We'll find out where you got the gun and what you did with it after you shot Dylan Renault in the back."

As far-fetched as Sam's theory was, Max couldn't ignore the fear seeping into him. Innocent people didn't get charged for crimes they didn't commit.

Did they?

SEVEN

Would she ever stop cringing at the sight of a police vehicle?

Ava's day had been stressful enough without pulling into her driveway and spying the sheriff's cruiser parked in the circle. The setting sun painted orange streaks against the blue backdrop of the sky. A breeze carried the hint of bayou on its wings.

Exhaustion took up residence in every muscle she had. After meeting with the department heads of the Renault Corporation and asking for department reports by Monday, she'd spent the afternoon working on Jocelyn's wedding. Reserve Reverend Harmon for the date, check. Order the flowers, check. Make arrangements for the wedding to take place outdoors, check. Order the cake and punch for the reception, check. Good progress, but Ava was drained. And now to come home to this.

She rested her forehead against the steering wheel and closed her eyes. If only she could go to sleep and wake up with all of this having been a bad dream.

But it wasn't a dream. None of it.

Lord, please give me strength.

She let out a moan, slung her designer bag higher on her shoulder, slammed the car door shut and made her way up the stairs.

Bosworth opened the door before she could reach for the knob. "Ms. Ava, Sheriff Reed is here to see Ms. Charla, but she refuses to talk to him. He said he'd wait for you." He shut the door firmly behind her, disapproval for the sheriff oozing from his every pore.

No escaping for her.

"Thank you, Bosworth." She set her purse on the foyer table.

"I sat him in the sitting room."

But of course, in the sitting room. Where else?

When would this dreadful ordeal end? It all wore her slap out—keeping up the family appearance, trying to go on with life, dealing with her mother's antics. With a sigh, she straightened her shoulders and entered the sitting room.

Sheriff Reed shoved to his feet. "Ms. Ava."

"What can I do for you, Sheriff?" The tiny thread of patience she had left threatened to snap.

"It's about Dylan's case."

Her heart hiccupped. They had to have questioned Max about the medallion by now. Had they found out something more? Maybe she'd get an answer to at least some of the questions keeping her mind warring with her heart. "Yes?" She struggled to remain composed as she took a seat on the Queen Anne wingback chair and crossed her legs at the ankles.

"We're working on figuring out what his last words meant."

Relief stormed through her, followed by a good dose of disappointment. Nothing about Max, but also no answers. "I'd like to know that as well, but as I've already told you, I haven't a clue what he meant."

"I understand that. But we'd like to rule out one possibility for sure."

"What's that?"

Sheriff Reed looked sheepish and wouldn't meet her eye.

"We'd like to rule out the possibility that he's the father of Sarah Farley."

All the air left Ava's lungs with a whoosh. It was one thing to wonder it herself, but to have the police question the possibility… She shook her head. "I don't understand."

"Just to rule out one angle we're looking into."

"Dylan never even dated Leah."

"Yes, ma'am, that's the general consensus, but it is possible, as she worked for your brother near the time she got pregnant."

"But Earl was Sarah's father."

"Could be that isn't totally accurate."

"He was Leah's husband." Her head hurt with the implications. "I don't see how any of this relates to Dylan's murder."

"Well, we're just trying to rule out possibilities." Sheriff Reed flipped pages in his notebook.

"What could it remotely have to do with my brother's murder? If he was Sarah's father, outlandish as that is." But the thought butted against her conscience. She, herself, had pondered the possibility.

"I'm not real sure, ma'am, but the FBI believes it's potentially linked to the other murders. We have to find a connection."

"I see." But she didn't. Was this just a tactic to smear her brother's name more than it already was? "What do you want from me?"

"I tried to talk to Mrs. Charla, but the maid said she still isn't feeling so good."

Ava smoothed her skirt. "Mother's taking Dylan's death very hard. I'm sure you can understand. He was her only son."

And Ava's only sibling.

"Yes, ma'am. But what we'd like is her authorization to use the samples taken from Dylan to run DNA testing against Sarah Farley."

She couldn't stop the gasp. "You kept samples of my brother?" Horror snaked along her spine.

A blush tinted the sheriff's cheeks. "Yes, ma'am. It's standard procedure to retain tissue, blood and organ samples during an autopsy."

Bile rose in the back of her throat. Standing on wobbly legs, she breathed in slowly, exhaling even slower. "I don't see what good this will do. Maybe you should just wait until Leah is found. I'm sure she knows who her daughter's father is."

"This paternity test will eliminate one of the theories revolving around motive and, well, um…you'd just know."

Ava didn't know Leah well, just in passing, but her heart ached for that poor little orphaned Sarah. Could the child be her niece?

But what if she wasn't? Would the gossip-mongering people of Loomis like Micheline Pershing ever let the speculation die if answers weren't provided? Proof-positive answers, at that. "And it'd put an end to the rumors, right?"

"Well, that, too, ma'am." At least he had the decency to avoid her gaze.

"I'll think about it and discuss it with Mother."

"I'd sure appreciate it."

"Bosworth will see you out." Ava rushed from the room, gestured to the butler hovering in the foyer and ran up the stairs to her private suite. She made it to the bathroom just in time to be sick.

Four hours in a small sheriff's interrogation room was enough to put anyone in a bad mood. For Max, it was beyond horrifying.

He'd made his call to the company lawyer more than an hour ago. How long did it take for him to talk to one of the other attorneys in the practice and send someone over? Fortunately, the FBI agent had left the room, leaving him alone with his thoughts.

And his fears.

Sheriff Reed swung open the door. "Mr. Tanner here to see you. Your lawyer." He nodded to the bald, thin man. "We'll give you fifteen minutes before we come back." He shut the door behind him.

Mr. Tanner extended his bony hand. "Mr. Pershing, I'm Lyle Tanner, an attorney in Carl's firm." He set a briefcase on the floor, withdrew a legal pad and plopped it on the table. "So, what've we got?"

Max filled the lawyer in on what had transpired. It was difficult to read the man—his expression never changed. Max would hate to be against him in a poker game. "So, they have an item of yours on the body and your meeting with him the week before the murder at the crime scene?"

"Yes."

"And the ongoing feud between your family and his?"

"Right."

Mr. Tanner laid his pen on his pad, lowered his glasses on the bridge of his nose and peered at Max over their rim. "I have to ask, Mr. Pershing, did you kill Dylan Renault?"

Max flexed his jaw muscles. "I most certainly did not."

The attorney stared until Max thought he'd turned to stone. Finally the man pushed his glasses back where they belonged. "I believe you."

Was there ever a question? What kind of lawyer was he?

"Now, tell me what they've said to you since you've been here and what you've stated. Don't leave anything out, no matter how minor. It could be legally important and a violation of your civil rights."

Okay, maybe he wasn't so bad after all.

Max relayed the conversations almost verbatim. When he

was done, the lawyer let out a heavy sigh. "Good, you haven't said anything that could incriminate you."

"But I didn't do anything, so how could I have incriminated myself?"

"Law enforcement can use whatever tactics they deem necessary to try to get a confession out of you. They can lie about evidence, circumstantial or physical, they can tell you lies about what people have told them… Pretty much, they can do whatever it takes to get you to confess."

"But a confession wouldn't be the truth. I didn't kill Dylan."

Lyle Tanner chuckled, surprisingly deep for his slight frame. "Mr. Pershing, they don't care about truth. They only care about solving their case. Period."

"Call me Max." He shook his head. "But they're focusing on me and not even looking for the real murderer."

"Call me Lyle. And you're right. But that happens all the time. Trust me, I've seen it all. I used to work at a large firm in Baton Rouge. You'd be amazed at the number of times I've seen innocent people charged with crimes while the real criminals go free."

"Are they cleared?" Max's heart raced.

"In some cases, yes. Sadly enough, not in all cases."

Now Max's gut clenched to the point of causing him to catch his breath. "So some people go to trial for something they didn't do?"

"Not just go to trial. Are convicted and sent to prison."

"How can that happen in this day and age?" The absurdity slammed against Max's conscience.

"Unfortunately, the way the laws are written, they basically give law enforcement free reign."

Outrageous. "So what do I do?"

"You answer their questions honestly. If it's a question I don't think you should answer, I'll touch your wrist."

"But why shouldn't I answer? I'm innocent."

Lyle sighed and shook his head. "Weren't you listening to me? It doesn't matter that you're innocent. They don't care. They only care about closing a case and what they think they can prove to a jury."

This was all moving way too fast. Very frightening to consider he could be charged and convicted of something he didn't do.

The conversation halted as the door to the interrogation room swung open. Sheriff Reed, Deputy Bertrand and Special Agent Sam Pierce waltzed in, forming almost a semicircle around Max and Lyle.

"Are you ready to talk now, Pershing?" Apparently, the FBI agent would head up the questioning.

"My client will answer your questions, Agent Pierce." Lyle Tanner exuded confidence.

"Fine." Sam turned his attention to Max. "Where were you between the hours of ten thirty and eleven thirty on January 23?"

Max swallowed hard. "Um, I was at work."

"In the office?"

"No, I had a meeting out of the office."

"Where and with whom?"

Max's gut tightened into a wad. "I was supposed to meet an appraiser, Denny Wren, at one of our properties on Merchant Street."

Sam cocked his head. "Supposed to?"

"Well—" Max licked his lips "—I was supposed to, but Denny never showed."

The sheriff and deputy both made notes. Not Agent Pierce. He continued to stare at Max. "So you were out of the office for how long?"

Max shrugged. "Maybe forty-five minutes or so."

"Why so long? Your office isn't that far from Merchant Street."

"I waited fifteen minutes for Denny before I realized he wasn't going to show. Since I didn't want to have the time totally wasted, I looked around and did my own calculations. Then I went back to the office."

"Can anyone collaborate your story?"

"I—I don't know. I—"

Lyle touched Max's wrist and interjected. "Mr. Pershing has stated where he was at the time of the murder. I do believe it's your responsibility as investigating officers to verify alibis, is it not?"

Sam didn't bother to answer the lawyer, just went right back in on Max. "You've identified the medallion as belonging to you. How did it come to be in the victim's pocket?"

Again, Lyle touched Max. "My client has already stated on the record that he doesn't know how Mr. Renault came into possession of the medallion."

"Why did you meet with the victim the week before his murder?"

Lyle jumped up from his chair. "These questions are redundant, Agent Pierce. Asked and answered on record." He slipped his notepad into his briefcase. "If you have nothing new to ask my client, either charge him or let him go."

Sam straightened, his jaw firm. "Don't leave town, Mr. Pershing."

Everyone seemed to be telling him that exact same advice. And never had he wanted to run away so badly.

EIGHT

How to broach the subject?

Ava paused outside her mother's door. She could only imagine Charla's reaction when she brought up the paternity test. More than likely, it'd cause another crying fit. While she didn't feel up to such after the long day she'd had, Ava didn't have much of a choice.

Dear Lord, please give me the words to approach this from the right angle.

She knocked softly. There was no response. She knocked again, harder this time. Still nothing.

A tendril of apprehension tickled between her shoulder blades.

The patio door slammed from the other side of Charla's suite. Ava started, then opened the door.

Bosworth, face flushed and thick, gray hair mussed, met her at the door. "Oh, Ms. Ava."

She glanced from Bosworth to her mother, sitting demurely in her wheelchair by the window. "Have you been outside, Mother?"

"What's wrong with getting a little fresh air?"

"Nothing." Certainly not. At least her mother was dressed appropriately and apparently getting out. "I'm glad to see you up and about."

"I'll just take your dinner tray to Bea." Bosworth lifted the sterling silver service and moved past Ava. He shut the door behind him.

Ava sat on the lounge.

"What do you want now, Ava?" Charla sounded tired and distracted. At least she wasn't yelling.

"Sheriff Reed came by today and—"

"What did he want? That man is incorrigible and a disgrace as a lawman. Why, the way he dogged my poor Dylan, thinking my son could have something to do with that…that gold digger's death…"

Oh, this wasn't going to go as well as Ava'd prayed. "He presented me with a solution to stop all the rumors going around town about Dylan and Leah." She swallowed, waiting for her mother to blow.

Charla didn't blow. She narrowed her eyes. "There was nothing between Dylan and that trash. Nothing."

"Mother, Leah was a nice girl, but that's beside the point."

"What does Bradford want?" Charla looked more like her regular self now than she had since Dylan had been shot.

"He wants your permission as next of kin to run some tests on samples taken during Dylan's a-a-autopsy." Even now, just thinking it, much less saying it, made Ava's stomach turn over.

Apparently, it didn't shock or sicken her mother. "What kind of tests?"

"A paternity test."

"What? A paternity test for what? On whom?"

Her mother wasn't this dense. She had to be shocked by the proposal. "On Sarah Farley."

"Leah and Earl's girl? Whatever for?"

"Mother, surely you know that because of Dylan's last words, speculation is that he's Sarah's father."

"That's ludicrous. Totally inconceivable." Charla's arms flailed like a pelican about to take flight.

"Have you seen Sarah Farley lately? She has the Renault eyes, Mother."

"There's no way she could. I can't believe you'd even consider such a possibility. As if your brother would stoop to fathering a child with that…that tramp."

"Mother!"

"Don't you *Mother* me, Ava Scarlet Renault! I won't allow any such test. Nothing will mar the Renault name, not even you."

Ava stood on shaky legs. "I'll give you time to adjust to the idea. Surel—"

"Get out. I'll not have this discussion anymore. I can't believe you'd even consider such a preposterous suggestion."

Ava walked to the door and left without another word. She made it down the hall and almost to the stairs when Bosworth stopped her. "Is Ms. Charla upset? I thought I heard her voice raised."

What, did he have radar tuned into the nuances of her mother's moods? No, it wasn't his fault. She offered a shaky smile. "She's upset with me. She'll be fine."

Bosworth's brows formed a firm line over his eyes. "I'll just go check on her."

"I wouldn't advise it, but be my guest." Ava turned and made her way up the stairs.

Once in her room, she threw herself across the bed and clutched a pillow to her chest. Her fists pounded the satin pillowcase.

Why, God? Why is this so hard?

With eyes pinched closed, little Sarah Farley's image filled her mind's eye. Blond hair—did it have a hint of strawberry in it, like Ava's? But her eyes…no denying they were the same shape and color as the trademark Renault eyes.

Just like Ava's and Charla's.

Ava bolted up and flung the pillow on the bed. If Sarah was Dylan's, then there was still a piece of her brother left. Could she live with not knowing the truth? But Charla had made it clear she'd never allow Dylan's samples to be tested.

She moved to her desk and booted up her laptop. Time to do a little online research to see what she could find out about DNA paternity tests.

Time to be proactive.

"What's this I hear about you working at Renault Corporation?" Lenore met him in the foyer, looking none too happy. Matter of fact, by the redness of her face and narrowed eyes, Max would take a guess that hot fury ran through her veins.

"I just helped Ava out for an afternoon." He tossed his keys on the buffet and let out a heavy sigh. He wasn't in the mood to deal with his mother tonight. But he'd have to tell her, so might as well get it over with, take a hot shower and forget this whole miserable day.

"And blew off your own job. What are you thinking, Max? You're my son and I love you to distraction, but sometimes you just don't think."

"Mom, come into the kitchen and have a drink with me. I have something to tell you."

Her eyes nearly popped out of her head before he turned and walked down the hall. Her heels clipped on the marble tile behind him. "What? Don't tell me you're involved with Ava Renault. Seriously, Maximilion, I don't think I can stand by and watch her destroy you again."

"It's not about Ava." He opened the fridge and pulled out a soft drink. He tilted it toward his mother.

"No, I don't want anything to drink. I want to know what's going on."

He bent over the center island, resting his elbows on the granite counter. "I'm the prime suspect in Dylan Renault's murder." There, he'd just thrown it out like casting a rod and reel. Now to wait for her to yank the bait.

"What? How on earth did this happen?"

Tired of the whole thing, Max relayed the events of his afternoon to his mother, downed his soda, then tossed the can in the trash.

"I'm calling Bradford. I can't believe he'd put my son through such nonsense. With nothing to go on."

"Mom, don't make it worse."

"How could I make this worse? You're a murder suspect. I don't know why Bradford didn't call me first."

"He couldn't. The FBI agent took charge of the investigation. Well, at least their questioning of me."

"All because of some stupid necklace Ava Renault told them was yours?" She stabbed the air in his direction. "See, this is just another reason why I want you to stay away from that girl. She ran to the FBI and pointed the finger at you."

"She didn't. They found the medallion on Dylan's body. Ava just identified it."

"But she told the police. If she's such a wonderful person, why didn't she ask you about it first?"

Now that was a good question. Why hadn't Ava asked him about the medallion?

Lenore was on a roll now, pacing, her heels clicking on the tile. "Oh, no. She sees the thing and can't wait to run and tell the FBI. What kind of woman does that? Especially when you just blew off your own company to help her with hers."

Wait a minute.

He held up his hand to his mother and strode toward the door.

She trailed him. "Max, where are you going?"

Grabbing his keys off the table, he marched to his car.

The 1999 red convertible Mercedes-Benz glistened in the security lights under the parking cover. He pressed the button on the fob and opened the car door. The car's automatic seat moved into his preset settings. A trace of Interlude perfume wafted past him. Pausing, he glanced over his shoulder at his mother. "Have you driven my car lately?" She was, after all, the only person besides him who had keys to it.

"Um, I drove it to the store that day my car was getting a tune-up."

It'd be nice if she'd let him know when she drove his car. Actually, it'd be nice if she asked beforehand.

He slipped into the driver's seat, flipped on the dome light and inspected the console. His gym membership card, two white golf tees and some loose change filled the area.

No medallion. No chain.

After getting back out of the car, Max slammed the door shut, hit the button to lock the doors and engage the security system and stormed toward the condo. So much for finding something. He'd just turned the knob when Sheriff Reed whipped into the lot.

The man barely had time to get out of the cruiser before Lenore got in his face. "I can't believe you'd question my son, Bradford. Make him feel like a murder suspect. What are you do—"

Gravel spinning on concrete, another deputy's car pulled into the parking area.

"What's going on here, Bradford?" Lenore's hands punched onto her hips.

The sheriff ignored Lenore, not even meeting her gaze, and headed toward Max. For years, Max had wondered if there was a romantic connection between his mother and the sheriff. Now, he certainly hoped not.

"Here's a warrant to search your condo, office and automobiles." He handed Max a folded group of papers. "Feel free to call Mr. Tanner. They're all complete."

"Who is Mr. Tanner, Max?" Lenore moved beside Max and snatched the papers from his hands.

"My attorney." Max nodded at the sheriff. "I'll go call him now."

He left with his mother still ranting and raving at Sheriff Reed. But all Max could think was how he was being set up. He hadn't a clue how the medallion got into Dylan's pocket—how it'd even gotten out of his car.

And for the life of him, he couldn't figure out why Ava hadn't asked him about it before telling the sheriff and FBI it was his.

She didn't need Charla's permission.

They could run the DNA test on her. Sure, it wasn't as conclusive and precise as using Dylan's DNA, but it would determine if Sarah and Ava were related.

But did Ava want to do that?

What if Sarah was her niece? Why hadn't her brother told her and their mother? Of course, considering her mother's reaction to Leah, Ava could understand Dylan not mentioning anything about her, if there'd been something. What went on between him and Leah? Why the secret? How could he have denied Sarah all her life, having her live right under their noses and not say a word?

Maybe she didn't know her brother as well as she'd like to believe.

To take the test or not?

Maybe Dylan hadn't known Sarah was his but he'd suspected and that's what he'd meant by his cryptic last words. Did Leah know? Had they argued? If so, then maybe she'd been the one to kill Dylan.

Except she was considered dead.

Ava shut her laptop and lay back out across the bed. The moon's light tickled past the curtains and sent beams across the ceiling.

What about Leah? If she knew Sarah was Dylan's, why had she married Earl? Maybe she'd tricked Earl into marrying her, then let him think the little girl was his. But why? The Renaults were the most affluent citizens of Loomis.

God, what do I do?

Ava rolled onto her stomach. The questions barraged her. If Sarah was Dylan's daughter, then she wanted to know. She had to know.

She sat upright and stared out the window into the bayou. She'd call Mr. Fayard tomorrow to see what the law had to say on these tests and what her options would be if the test proved positive that she and Sarah were related.

A breeze blew the curtains open. Across the way, Ava could make out Pershing Plaza.

Max.

She leaned forward, resting her forearms against the windowsill. How did Max play into all this? Why had he given his medallion to Dylan? Nothing made sense. She was too confused to ask Max about it yet.

The sound of a woman shouting carried on the breeze. Ava stilled, listening. It sounded like …

Ava opened the window more and stuck her head against the screen.

Yep, it was Lenore Pershing's gravelly voice shouting. Who was she lighting into? Hopefully, not Max.

No, she shouldn't care. She didn't care.

Ava slammed the window shut and moved to the bathroom to remove her makeup.

Once in her pajamas, she updated her notes on Jocelyn's

wedding, with a memo to herself to call Cathy in the morning to finish up all the little things left. It looked like the wedding would go off without a hitch.

The investigation wasn't so lucky.

The evidence seemed to mount against Max. On one hand, she just couldn't believe Max capable of murdering anyone, much less someone who meant a lot to her. But how'd Dylan get Max's medallion, and have it on him when he died? And their meeting the week before …

Now that she thought about it, Max sure seemed eager to jump in and help her at the Renault Corporation. Was it possible the Pershing business was in financial trouble? Could Max have killed Dylan, then offered to help her in order to gain access to the Renault Corporation's finances?

No, Max wouldn't do such a thing. Never. Despite the evidence.

Or was that just her heart's wishful thinking?

NINE

The sun crested over the trees behind Renault Mansion, casting splays of light between the pines and cypress trees of the bayou. Little beams caught in the branches, twinkling like diamonds in the rough. Ava stared out the window, marveling at God's creation all around her. After a restless night, she reveled in the tranquility of this beautiful Saturday morning. She lifted her coffee cup and took a sip of the strong brew. A distinct hum reached her ears, and she turned from the window.

Charla had her wheelchair on its highest speed, racing into the dining room. "Have you seen this?" She stopped beside Ava and slammed the *Loomis Gazette* onto the table. Rhett startled at the thump.

"Good morning, Mother." She struggled not to register surprise over seeing Charla out of her suites.

"Just look at the front page," Charla snapped.

What now? Ava lifted the paper and popped it open. Her eyes scanned the headlines, and her heart jumped.

Business Rivalry Gone Too Far?
Max Pershing Implicated in Murder of Dylan Renault

* * *

Oh, no.

"Read it. Read all about how that vile Pershing killed your brother." Charla crossed her arms over her chest.

Ava's stomach knotted as she scanned the article.

Loomis, La.—Family feud gone too far? Sheriff Bradford Reed gave a statement early this morning that through the combined effort of the Loomis Sheriff's office and assisting FBI investigators, evidence recovered at the scene of Dylan Renault's murder has been identified as belonging to Maximilion "Max" Pershing.

Pershing, 32, is the major stockholder of Pershing Company, with subsidiaries of Pershing Land Developing and Pershing Real Estate.

Sheriff Reed further stated that Pershing met with the victim at the scene of the crime the week before the murder occurred, with no logical explanation given. Furthermore, Pershing has no alibi for the time of the murder.

The Pershing family, who has long been at odds with the Renault family, made no statement.

Closing the newspaper, Ava stared at her mother. "I just can't believe Max would be involved in Dylan's murder."

Charla's eyes narrowed. "It's just like those Pershings... cowards. Shooting my boy in the back."

Ava had to admit—the way the article was written, all the evidence pointed to Max. And it was new to her that Max didn't have an alibi.

"This is a prime example of why I refused to let you date that dirty rat. He's a killer." Charla's voice rose.

"Mother, I don't think Max murdered anyone, much less Dylan."

"Why would you defend him? Against your brother?" Charla glared. "What kind of woman are you that you wouldn't care that he murdered your brother—shot him in the back in cold blood?"

"I know Max. He couldn't have done such a thing." But the evidence sure looked convincing.

Charla wheeled around so fast that poor little Rhett almost fell off her lap. "You *know* Max? How about knowing your brother? How about demanding justice for his murder?"

"Oh, I want the person who killed Dylan to answer for his crime. I just don't think that person is Max."

A heavy pause filled the air.

"How dare you defend the man who killed your brother? I raised you better than this." Charla's voice reached the level of shouting, something Ava hadn't heard from her in years. "I will not tolerate such disrespect. Not in my own home." Her face turned as red as the buoys on the other side of the swamp.

"Calm down, Mother. Your blood pressure—"

"Forget my blood pressure. You're a traitor."

Bosworth stormed into the doorway, then halted with a jerk. "Charla!"

She turned in the chair to glare at him.

Ava held her breath. She'd never in her life seen the servant speak in such a way to her mother.

Charla wagged a finger. "This isn't any of your concern, Jon."

"But you're too upset. You should retire to your room to rest."

"Rest? When my own daughter is turning traitor? How can I rest?"

"Mother, I'm not a traitor. I'm just after the truth. All the police have is circumstantial evidence and a theory that Max was involved."

Charla huffed. "Evidence is evidence."

"Ma'am, please. Let me escort you back to your suites. I'll have Bea make you a cup of tea." Bosworth's face was wreathed in worry and concern.

Her mother hesitated a moment, then nodded at him. As he moved to stand beside her, Charla made a final statement. "Ava, you stay away from those Pershings. I mean it."

Ava clamped her lips together as Bosworth and her mother crossed out of the dining room and headed down the hall. Their voices were mere murmurs with the hum of the wheelchair.

Could it be true? *Could* Max have been involved? Everyone else seemed to think so—her mother, the sheriff, even the newspaper reporter. Was it possible she was letting her emotions blind her to the truth? The evidence?

Perhaps. But she had another issue to deal with first.

Leaving her now-cooled coffee, Ava made her way into the office and closed the door. She dialed the number for Paul Fayard, realizing he most likely wasn't in the office on a Saturday, but she wanted to leave a message. If she didn't, she just might change her mind, and she needed to know the legal ramifications of the situation.

Waiting for the voice mail to click on, Ava flipped through the inventory sheet of Dylan's personal things the deputy had left with her. She scanned it first, something niggling that didn't seem right, but she couldn't figure out what.

The message came on and Ava asked Mr. Fayard to return her call as early as possible to answer some legal questions she had which had nothing to do with the Renault Cooperation. She hung up the phone. Actually, that wasn't quite right. If Sarah was proven to be Dylan's daughter, then she was a legal heir of the Renault fortune.

Ava's world was crashing down around her, and there wasn't a thing she could do about it.

Except demand answers.

She retrieved the paper from the dining room table and snagged her keys from the foyer. It was time to just expose everything. Lay it all on the line.

And the only way to do that was to talk to Max.

It was time for the truth.

No rest for the weary.

Lenore had shown up at his condo bright and early. So much for a lazy Saturday sleep-in day. The sheriff's office had gone through the condo until the wee hours of the morning. The place was trashed.

Now, Max had awoken to his mother clanking around in the kitchen. He dragged himself to the bathroom, stepping over the emptied drawers and piles of his stuff, courtesy of the Loomis parish sheriff's office, and stood under a fast burst of hot water.

His mother meant well—her heart was in the right place. Tragic events called for comfort food, that was her motto. He could expect the full gamut when he tromped downstairs. Eggs over easy, bacon, toast, orange juice and coffee. But she'd also pick at his insecurities while he ate. Been there and done that one too many times. The only break he'd gotten in her regimen was the five years spent at LSU in Baton Rouge.

As he shaved, his thoughts went to Ava. What could she be thinking right now? That she'd taken the information about the medallion being his to the police before even asking him said a lot. Despite the old feelings beginning to blossom again, he couldn't believe she'd turn him over to the police. First chance he got, he intended to discuss the situation with her.

"Max!"

He pulled on jeans and a sweater from a stack on the floor before trudging down the stairs in his bare feet. "I'm coming, Mom."

"Breakfast is ready."

As if he couldn't tell by the hickory scent of the bacon and strong aroma of the coffee. He slouched into the kitchen and dropped into a chair. The kitchen was back in order. His mother's doing, of course. She might not have any taste in decor, but Lenore Pershing couldn't stand disorder.

She sat a plate in front of him, precisely between the cup of coffee and glass of concentrated orange juice. One hundred percent predictable. "I still can't believe Bradford would think you had anything to do with the murder of that hapless playboy." She passed him the salt and pepper.

Digging right in before his first sip of coffee—he hated to be right on target all the time. Of course, where his mother was concerned, it wasn't exactly rocket science. "I guess he's just doing his job."

"His job?" She huffed.

"The FBI is probably directing him." For a moment, Max felt sorry for the sheriff. He and Lenore went way back—back to when Lenore's husband, Max's father, ran off and divorced her decades ago—and the sheriff always seemed to be sweet on her. Sometimes to the point where Max wondered if they'd had a special relationship when he was younger and not so observant.

"Well, he should be man enough to stand up to them. He lives here. He's known you since you were a child. There's no way he can believe you'd be involved."

The bacon was too done. Crisp wasn't the way Max liked it. He swallowed hard, the hickory-flavored edges scraping against his throat. "I don't know, Mom. All I know is I'm innocent and I think I'm being framed."

"Framed?" She set her coffee cup on the table with a thump. The brown liquid sloshed over the rim. "How on earth are you being framed?"

"Someone put that medallion in Dylan's pocket. Why else would they do that except to implicate me?"

"Why?"

He shook his head. "I haven't a clue, except to make me look like a murderer. Maybe because it's a well-known fact that the Pershings and Renaults don't get along."

His mother's face paled. "Who would do such a thing?"

"I don't know, but I aim to find out." He swigged the orange juice, washing out the taste of the charred toast. Poor Lenore, she'd never been much of a cook.

Her face brightened. "It had to be Ava."

He choked on the juice and coughed. Max swallowed, coughed again then took a sip of the coffee. "Ava? Are you serious?"

"Why not? She's the one who went running to the police about the medallion being yours in the first place. Why wouldn't she set you up?" She wiped imaginary crumbs from the place mat in front of her. "Think about it…maybe she had this all planned for some time. Didn't you say she's now taking over the Renault Corporation?"

He needed a map to keep up with her train of thought. "What's that have to do with anything?"

"What if she wanted control of the corporation and couldn't get it with Dylan around?" Lenore creased her nose. "Maybe she killed Dylan, realized what she'd done, panicked, and needed someone to set up for the crime."

"But me?" And Ava would no more kill her brother than, well, he would.

"Of course, you. Y'all had recently begun working together on the pageant committee and were talking again. She was getting back in your good graces. Had it all planned so you wouldn't suspect her." Lenore stood and carried her cup to the sink. "It makes perfect sense. I told you she was trying to get her hooks back into you. Here's why."

As strange and deranged as it sounded, he could almost follow her logic. Maybe Ava *had* orchestrated everything—their being on the committee together, getting their relationship on a more friendly footing…yeah, he could see that. But to have killed her brother? No way, no how.

"I think you're way off base, Mom. Ava wouldn't kill her brother."

"You'd be surprised what people will do, Maximilion."

"For what possible reason?"

"Greed. Money. Power." Lenore grabbed her purse from the counter. "She is, after all, Charla's daughter. Who knows what poison that woman's infected her children with."

Max set his dishes in the sink and faced his mother. "Ava's not like that."

Lenore smiled but looked sad. "You're still remembering the young woman you fell in love with back in high school, son. Back before Charla taught her the wicked ways of the world." She shook her head. "Don't fall for it. You'd be a fool not to remember how she just wrote you off without even so much as an explanation."

Ava had avoided him up until last month.

The week before Dylan had been murdered.

His mother stood on tiptoe and planted a kiss on his jaw. "I have some errands to do in town, but I'll have a cleaning service here by this afternoon to put your place back in order."

"Thank you."

She moved toward the door, then paused. "Are you going to church with me in the morning?"

He let out a dry laugh. "Mom, I haven't gone to church with you in years. Why do you keep asking?"

"Because I refuse to give up on your eternal salvation."

"You don't get anything out of the service. You only go to catch up on gossip and see who's wearing what."

"What a tacky thing to say." But she smiled as she let herself out.

Max ran water over the dishes and placed them in the dishwasher. His thoughts raced in twenty different directions.

Ava.

Could she have set him up? It was still too much for him to swallow that she killed her own brother, but maybe once the deed had been done, she saw her opportunity. No, that wasn't Ava.

Yet she'd rushed in and taken over the corporation, even though she hadn't a clue about the investment business or how to run the family empire. And she'd sure jumped on his offer to help her. Could his mother be right? Could Ava be so like her mother?

No, she was kind and gentle. A delicate rose amid a family of thorns. The meaning of the medallion she'd given him. They were two roses in the midst of their thorny families. Or was he the only rose and Ava had become the thorn in his side? The thorn that wanted to see him put away for a murder he didn't commit.

TEN

Good, both his car and truck were here. That meant Max was home.

Ava took a long breath, curtailing her anxiety, fear and anger all rolled into a tight ball in the center of her stomach. She needed to curb her emotions and be rational.

As if she'd ever been able to string coherent thoughts together around Max. He had a knee-weakening effect on her, just by being in close proximity. Which was one of the reasons she'd avoided him when he returned to Loomis from LSU. After her mother and Dylan told her about some business deals in which the Pershings got clients to invest in real estate instead of with the Renault Corporation, Ava promised her parents she'd steer clear of Max.

And then there was the secret of her past.

But now…she had no other choice but to confront him.

Lord, I could really use some divine wisdom and guidance right about now.

She tucked the newspaper under her arm and rang the doorbell. Her heart rose into her throat.

The door swung open, and Max filled the doorway. Filled the doorway with his over-six-foot frame. His wide shoulders. His dark, wavy hair still damp from the shower. His jeans and sweater. Okay, he filled the doorway, and her senses, with a grabbing reality. No man should look so good first thing on a Saturday morning.

"Ava." He ground out her name, as if it hurt to pronounce it.

The speech she'd mentally prepared on the drive over flew right out of her head. She slapped the newspaper against his chest. "I want an explanation."

Pain flickered in his eyes, followed immediately by anger, an emotion she wasn't used to seeing from him. "I'd like one as well. Actually, I think I'm entitled to one."

"You? An explanation for what, pray tell?"

He motioned her inside, glancing over her shoulder. "I'd rather not have this discussion on my front doorstep, if you don't mind."

She stomped into his condo and immediately wished she hadn't. Never had she been in Max's private space before. The entire area seemed to swallow her in Max's pure essence. The smell of his cologne. The art an extension of his good taste, which was in direct contrast to the gaudiness of the building's exterior. The plush carpet that seemed to wrap around her feet. She wanted to kick off her flats and bury her toes in the lushness.

Moving from the foyer, she spied the living room. A warm, brown leather couch and recliner faced a fireplace with a mounted television over the mantel. But the mess—things thrown everywhere as if he'd been searching for something in a great hurry.

"Excuse the mess. The Loomis parish sheriff's office helped me with some redecorating last night." Max's tone was pure sarcasm. What was he talking about?

"Come on into the kitchen. Coffee's still hot." He moved around her, leading the way.

She studied his back as he walked, his muscles rippling under his thin sweater. Suddenly, even the thought of coffee made her stomach recoil.

He poured coffee, then turned to her. "Still add a little coffee to your sugar and milk?"

She nodded, touched that he remembered after all these years, and took a seat at the dinette table tucked into the bay window alcove. Max had a nice home. Her heart thudded. At one time, she'd planned to have a home with Max.

He set a steaming cup in front of her before taking a seat across the table, then opened the newspaper. His eyes darted back and forth for a few seconds. He set the paper down with a sigh. "I'm sure you know exactly what evidence they've recovered."

"The necklace." Her throat threatened to close.

"Yes. The one *you* told them was mine."

"It is yours, Max. I gave it to you the night…"

"The night you left. The night you swore to wait on me."

Regret filled her chest, and she broke eye contact to stare into her cup. She took in a steadying breath before looking back at him. "Yes. That's the night I gave it to you. What I'd like to know is how it got in my brother's pocket the day he was murdered."

"I'd like to know the same thing."

She stared into his eyes, searching for confirmation of the truth, detection of falsehood, anything. Nothing jumped out at her. How could she have known every nuance of his face so well fifteen years ago and not be able to tell if he was lying now? "If you don't know how it got there, try telling me why you kept it."

"Because you gave it to me. It was proof that you loved me." His gaze slid to the floor as his voice cracked.

Guilt held her voice hostage. She could only stare back at him with pain thrumming through her veins.

"Let me ask you this, Ava—why did you take it to the sheriff before talking to me about it?"

Her voice cracked, but at least she could speak. "I saw it when the deputy brought by Dylan's personal belongings. I was shocked, to say the least, to see it again. Touch it. Naturally, the deputy picked up on my reaction and questioned me." He thought she'd found it on her own and run to the sheriff? Could he really think her so low?

"So, you didn't mean to point the finger at me?"

"Of course not." Then again, this *was* a murder investigation they were talking about. Her brother's murder. "I would've told them anyway, but I probably would've asked you about it first." At least she *thought* she would have.

Relief flitted across his face. "Can I ask you something else?"

"Yes." Unless it was about the past.

"Why did you want to take over the Renault Corporation?"

"I refuse to let the company that was my grandfather's, that Dylan put so much time and energy into building, just die. I owe it to their memories to keep it going." And if Dylan had an heir, to protect the company for her. "Why did you offer to help me?"

He paused and took a long sip of his coffee. She waited, wondering if he was delaying to think up an excuse.

"Honestly?"

"Yes. I want the truth."

"Because I could be close to you."

Ouch. That one hit her smack in the face. "Oh." What more could she say to that?

In an instant, his hands were over hers. "Ava, there are some things in our past we need to discuss, but you need to know this—I didn't kill your brother. I wasn't involved with his murder in any way, shape or form." He squeezed her hands before withdrawing his own. "And it really hurts that you could even think, for one second, that I could've done this."

She felt lower than the scum sitting on the swamp. Her heart had told her he couldn't be involved, yet the evidence… "What about you not having an alibi for the time of the murder?"

"I went out to look at some property, meeting an appraiser. He didn't show. I didn't want it to be a total waste of my time so I had a look around."

"What about that meeting with Dylan the week before his murder? Come on, Max. You have to admit it doesn't even sound right." *Please, please have a logical answer.* One she could believe and cling to.

He nodded. "I don't know why he asked for my opinion. Maybe because he knew I wouldn't tell anyone. I don't know. I wish I'd never met with him. But I did, and I'm telling the truth about what we discussed. That's all I know."

"So how do you explain the medallion being in his pants pocket?"

"I think I'm being framed."

"Framed?" Ava's eyes widened more than his mother's had. The difference being, Max was held spellbound by the honest beauty in Ava's face. "Why would you think that?"

"It's the only logical explanation for how the medallion got in Dylan's pocket." And he truly hoped Ava wasn't involved in setting him up. Now that he knew about the deputy being there when she saw and identified the medallion, her motive for taking over at the Renault Corporation…well, he could see her total innocence.

"But how? Who?"

"I don't know who, and I don't exactly know how. But someone took that medallion and planted it in Dylan's pocket. That person had to be the murderer."

"You don't think someone gave it to Dylan before he even showed up there? He could've gotten it early that morning and slipped it into his pants pocket."

She had a point. He pushed aside his cup. "I never considered that. But still, if I'm being framed, someone had to know Dylan was going to be murdered to give him the medallion."

"But that could mean you aren't being framed. That it's just bad timing." Sincerity cloaked her features. Those amazing Renault eyes.

"Then how can you explain away someone even having my medallion?"

"Where was the last place you know you had it?"

"At Clancy's Gym, about a month ago. I'd been playing racquetball and the chain broke. After my shower, I took it and put it in my car console so I could get to the jeweler's and get another chain if that one couldn't be repaired."

"And did you take it to the jeweler's?"

He shook his head, trying to remember. "By the time I got out of the gym, it was late. The jeweler was closed. I left it in my car's console."

"Did you take it maybe the next day?"

"No. I've been driving my truck." He flashed her a sheepish grin. "I don't like taking the car out in cold and nasty weather."

She grinned. "I can imagine." The smile slid from her face. "Is it possible that maybe the necklace didn't make it into your car at all? Maybe you dropped it as you were getting in?"

"I saw it. I remember the end of the chain almost caught on the gearshift."

"But did you see the medallion, not the chain, once you put it in the car? Maybe the charm fell off and someone picked it up."

He closed his eyes, fighting to recall that particular evening. "I'd lost the game, I remember that. The chain somehow broke and it slid to the floor." He concentrated harder. "I picked it up and the medallion was still on the chain. I went into the locker room and put it on the shelf by my wallet."

"Who were you playing with?"

Max stared at her. "I've tried to remember, but can't. I plan on calling my regular guys on Monday to see if any of them remember."

"Okay. So you put it in your locker."

"Right." He focused again. "I got dressed and grabbed my wallet and the chain and my keys."

"Was the medallion on the chain then?"

He paused, trying to picture the moment. He recalled putting his wallet into the pocket of his jeans. Could feel the cold of the keys against his palm. Could feel the weight of the chain in his hand. But was the medallion there?

"I can't remember."

"Okay, let's just say it was. What did you do next?"

"I headed out to my car." But stopped. "Wait. I stopped at the front desk to check the reservation of the court for later in that week."

"Did you set the necklace down?"

Had he? He knew he'd used a finger to glance at the appointment book, but was the chain in his hand? "I don't know."

"Let's say you didn't for the sake of argument. What'd you do then?" Ava leaned her elbows on the table.

"I went out to my car and put the necklace in the console. The end of the chain almost got caught on the gearshift, I remember that, so I had to make sure it was in the console."

"And you don't remember if the medallion was on there?"

Why could he see the chain so clearly in his mind, but not the medallion?

"I don't."

"And did you see the necklace again after that?"

"No. I haven't driven my car since. After the sheriff questioned me, I came home and checked, and the medallion isn't there." He shook his head. "And neither is the chain. But I *know* I saw it in the console."

"So, from what you told me, the medallion could've fallen off when you put the chain in your locker, or when you were at the front desk, or even on the way to your car. Right?"

"Yeah."

"Someone could've found it and picked it up. It has my name on it, so it's pretty obvious whose it was."

"Right."

"And that someone could've actually meant to give it to me, but forgot. Or they don't know me."

"Or were scared to approach you."

She shot him an inquiring look.

He raised his hands in mock surrender. "Hey, I'm just saying your name alone can intimidate some people."

"Whatever." She flipped her shiny hair over her shoulder. He could almost remember the satiny feel against his hand. "So weeks pass and they find the medallion again or remember. If they're intimidated by me, or don't know me, maybe they know Dylan. From the golf course or something."

"I'm following you."

"They give it to him, telling him they found it and thinks it belongs to me."

"Okay. So far it's logical."

"He recognizes the quality because our family's used the same jeweler for years. He sees my name, figures it's mine and slips it into his pocket to give me at home. No one trying to set you up."

"Don't you find it a bit coincidental they happen to return it the exact day he's shot?"

Her pretty features twisted. "Hang on a minute. I'm trying to remember something."

She was so cute when trying to concentrate. Her eyebrows bunched up and her nose wrinkled. Her fingers toyed with the neck of her shirt.

She slammed her hands to the table, eyes wide and face paling by the second.

His heart felt like a knife had just sliced through it. "What?"

"Max, you were right. Someone is trying to set you up."

Heart pounding, he reached across the table and took her hands in his. "After all the over-explaining you just did? Why do you say that?"

"Because the inventory sheet says the medallion was found in Dylan's front pants pocket."

Where was she going with this? "So?"

"His left front pocket. Dylan was right-handed. And besides, ever since he had carpal tunnel surgery on his left hand a couple of years ago, it was weakened. Dylan *never* put anything in his left front pocket. *Ever.* If someone gave him the medallion, he'd have automatically put it in his right front pocket, not his left." The color had totally vanished from her face. "Someone either saw you drop it or took it from your car and put it in Dylan's pocket to frame you."

ELEVEN

Now, beyond any doubt, Ava knew her heart had been right about Max. The relief and reassurance warmed her all the way to her toes.

"Now we have to figure out who and why."

She nodded, realizing he still held her hands. No wonder her thoughts were so jumbled. "I'd say the killer."

"Definitely, because they had to put the medallion on him after shooting him."

She shivered. Someone would be so cold to shoot her brother and then plant evidence to incriminate Max. Who would be so bold, so hateful? Slowly, she pulled her hands into her lap. She wouldn't be able to think clearly while he touched her.

"Do you think that means all of this was premeditated?"

Ava pondered the possibilities. "I'd think it'd have to be. I mean, they had to get Dylan to the property, have a gun on them or within easy access, and have the medallion with them to plant it."

"I think so, too." Max let out a heavy sigh and ran a hand over his dark waves.

She remembered how soft they were to her touch and shook her head. She needed to concentrate, not waltz down Memory Lane.

"So we're back to square one—who murdered Dylan?"

Max rubbed his hand over his chin. "You know, maybe Dylan told us who shot him. Maybe it was 'Sarah's father.'"

"What? Earl was already dead. How could he have shot Dylan?"

"Talk around town is that Earl wasn't Sarah's father."

A vise tightened around her heart. "No, rumor is Dylan was."

"But what if neither man was Sarah's father?"

That jerked her head upright. "What do you mean?"

"What if Dylan knew Sarah's real father, and it wasn't Earl or him? Maybe that's what he was trying to tell the FBI."

She hadn't considered that possibility. Hmm… "But who else could be Sarah's father? We can't exactly ask Leah."

"I think that's the question we need to be asking. Obviously, it was vitally important to Dylan or he wouldn't have wasted his dying breath trying to tell us."

"You're saying if we find out who Sarah's father is, we'll likely find who killed my brother?"

He nodded. "It's the most logical place to start, wouldn't you say?"

But there was a chance Dylan was Sarah's father. No denying the child resembled Charla and Ava herself.

And Ava had the power to find out.

Yet, she didn't feel up to sharing all of this with Max just yet. It was too personal, too private. Plus, she needed to wait to hear what Mr. Fayard said where the law stood on the issue. The attorney's words came back to her. "What about the evidence?"

"What evidence? All they have is my medallion, which puts me at the top of their suspect list."

"The long red hairs found on Earl's and Dylan's clothes—they're a match with each other and, from what I recently learned, come from a red wig. A wig that's made from natural hair."

"Hairs?" Max's brows lowered. "What hairs?"

"You don't know? How can you not know this?"

"Tell me."

She filled him in on the particulars—red, not strawberry blond, long, and definitely from a human.

He leaned back in his chair. "I'm not redheaded, so why am I such a prime suspect? And this links the murders together. This should clear me." He shoved to his feet, pacing the confines of the kitchen like a tiger in a cage. "They didn't even tell me."

Typical. She'd learned back when Dylan was a suspect in Angelina's murder that law officials didn't exactly play fair. "But it's a wig. Maybe they thought you could've put one on."

He snorted and slammed the side of his fist against the kitchen island. "I didn't even know about the hairs." He shook his head. "Maybe that's what they were looking for when they trashed my place. A stupid, red wig."

While she figured out what to do with the DNA test, they could work the wig angle. "Okay, why the red wig?"

"Why a wig, period? What's the tie-in?"

"And let's not forget about Sarah's reaction to people with red hair."

"What're you talking about?"

She let out a sigh. He truly was out of the loop. "Jocelyn worked with Sarah after Earl's murder and Leah's disappearance. They believe she saw something, and it had to be someone with red hair because of her reactions."

"You're thinking all the murders are connected?"

"It makes the most sense."

"But with a wig involved, it could be anybody."

Think, Ava, think outside the box. "Let's back up a minute. Back to the first murder."

"Earl's." Max returned to his seat, peering at her intently.

"Right. That's what Jocelyn believes Sarah saw. Or at least something related to his murder."

"Okay. So Earl's killer wore the red wig."

"Right." But something else occurred to her. "Or maybe not."

He cocked his head. "I'm not following you."

"What if the person who killed Earl is really a redhead?"

His forehead wrinkled. "But the wig…"

She shook her head, her thoughts tumbling over one another. "We're talking about someone who's killed four people so far, and had to have at least some reason and planning, right?"

"Okay. Still not seeing your point."

"I'm getting there. Bear with me." She struggled to bring her jumbled thoughts into cohesiveness. It didn't help that Max pierced her with his all-seeing eyes. "This redhaired person kills Earl. The police figure he set it up to look like a suicide. Why couldn't the killer have planted the hairs from the wig to distract from him?"

Max paused, squinting. "I can see that. But why a red wig? Wouldn't he use another color so as not to be a suspect?"

"That's my point exactly! Wouldn't it throw everyone off more if a redhead was planting evidence of a red wig?"

His eyes widened. He got it. "Someone would have to be very crafty and slick to think of that."

"Any more than killing four people and getting away with it?" She was on to something—she felt it. Excitement stirred in her chest.

"True."

"This person is clever. They've been able to stay a step ahead of the FBI, not just Sheriff Reed, so they're crafty."

He nodded, that spark of enthusiasm flickering in his eyes.

"Used it for distraction." Her own veins were filled with exhilaration.

"Right. So someone is a very smart planner."

Before she could respond, his phone rang. Loudly. He jumped up and grabbed the cordless from the counter. "Hello."

His eyes immediately clouded, and his expression went slack. Something wasn't good.

"I'm kind of in the middle of something right now. Can you ask them to come later?" He let out a sigh. "No, nothing like that. Sure. Thanks, Mom." A beep sounded as he replaced the phone on its base.

Lenore. Ava should've known. "Everything okay?"

"She's hired some housekeepers to come by and put my place back in order." He didn't sit back down.

"When?"

"They're on their way now."

Which ended their conversation. Ava stood. "I have some things to take care of anyway." Like doing some more praying about the DNA test.

He grabbed her hand. "We need to finish this discussion. We're on the right track." He smiled, and her insides melted.

"Let's keep thinking of redheaded people in town. Between the two of us, we should know everyone."

Laying a hand on her shoulder, Max drew her closer even as she made her way toward the foyer. "Right."

At the door, she turned to stare into his face. It was her undoing. Her tongue tied into a jillion knots. "I'll, uh, call you, uh, later."

He brushed her hair behind her ear. So intimate, and so familiar. Her heart pounded as he lowered his head and grazed a kiss across her temple. "And once we figure all this out, you and I need to discuss some more personal issues."

Words escaped her. They always had when his lips touched her. She nodded, then rushed to the parking lot.

What a fine mess she'd landed in now.

* * *

Redheads, redheads—who knew Loomis had so many of them?

Max sat at the dinette table, shoving down a quick lunch of a ham and cheese po'boy and making a list of all the people he knew who had red hair. His concentration kept being interrupted by the cleaning crew. He forced himself to review the names he'd jotted.

First was Vera Peel. Even though she'd owned the boarding house in town for as long as Max could remember, the woman creeped him out. Snapped at people. His mother had never liked her, but what did that mean? Years ago, Vera's husband had run off with another woman. Vera had stayed in Loomis, just getting more and more rude as time wore on. But Max couldn't quite picture her running around killing people. She'd been angry for years—why start killing townsfolk now? And the victims were all young, with no apparent connection to Vera. Max kept her on the list but drew a line through her name.

He next wrote down the name of Shelby Mason, Loomis librarian. She had long, red hair, but she was Leah's best friend. What motive could she possibly have to kill Leah and Earl? Not to mention, Max didn't think she had any connection to Angelina or Dylan. But she fit the profile he'd created in his mind.

Angelina and Dylan had been rumored to be a steady couple despite everyone knowing Dylan enjoyed his playboy status. There was even a rumor that Angelina expected an engagement ring. Earl and Leah were married. Maybe he should consider the fact that two involved couples were murdered and see if he could find a link between the couples.

Vera didn't run with the young crowd. She didn't even run with the older crowd. Now that Max thought about it, Vera didn't really have any friends that he knew of. He'd have to ask his mother. But just because no one liked her didn't mean she was a killer.

Back to Shelby. Maybe she and Leah had a falling out. Maybe about Sarah's paternity, which would involve Earl. Maybe she'd had a crush on Dylan no one knew about.

Max shook his head. He was grasping at straws, desperate for something solid. Anything to go on.

"Mr. Pershing?" One of the cleaning crew, a twenty-something blond girl, stood in the kitchen entryway.

"Yes?"

"I just wanted to let you know how sorry I am this happened to you."

Max squinted and stared. Did he know her? She didn't look very familiar to him. "Thank you."

She nodded, but didn't move from the doorway. "I'm praying for you."

What? Who *was* this girl? "I'm sorry, but do I know you?"

"Not really. I work for Reverend Harmon. I clean the church."

Well, that explained her praying for him statement. "I see."

She still didn't go away. Only cocked her head to the side and continued to stare. Strange girl. Not wanting to continue this conversation, Max went back to his list and noticed something he'd unconsciously done.

He'd been listing the women with red hair first. Because Ava had told him the hairs found had been long, indicative of a female. But now that they knew the hair came from a wig, the killer could be a man with short hair. Didn't that go along with Ava's profile of the killer being crafty and trying to throw the police off even more by wearing a woman's wig?

Felt like a distinct possibility.

Chuck Peters had red hair. Max swallowed the chuckle. The man was a drunk—always had been, always would be. No way he could have had anything to do with any of the murders, much less participated and not gotten caught. Max drew a line through his name.

That left Bartholomew Hansen. He had red hair. Max didn't know much about him but could probably find out scads from his mother. And Earl had fought with Bartholomew Hansen at the Christmas tree lighting in Loomis Park. Hmm. That could be a connection. Max had helped break up the fight, which had made Earl madder than a coon dog retired from hunting.

That only left one redhead. Georgia Duffy.

Max glanced up and froze. The blond girl still stood in the doorway, just staring at him as if in a trance. The way she stared…it unnerved him. He cleared his throat. "Was there something else?"

She focused on him. "Mr. Pershing, please don't think me rude or nosy, but I just remember my mother telling me how active you once were in the church. I can't help but wonder what happened."

He really didn't want to have this conversation, period. Especially not now with this girl he didn't know. "Let's just say God and I aren't exactly on speaking terms these days."

"Because you feel like He let you down?"

Little pinpricks of apprehension trailed their way down his back. "Something like that."

She nodded, as if he'd given the answer she expected. "You know, Mr. Pershing, Proverbs 3 says, 'Trust in the Lord with all your heart, and lean not on your own understanding.' For some reason, I just felt led to share that with you." With another smile, she was gone.

He stared at the empty space she'd just occupied. Who was she to quote Scripture to him? Didn't he know so many verses from heart, having them drilled into him at Sunday school and summer Bible camp? For years he'd read his Bible at least twice a day, drawing strength from God's promises. But there'd been no follow-through on those promises.

Max had cried out to God to bring Ava back to him, yet his prayers had fallen on deaf ears.

Or had they? She was back in his life now. Could his prayers have been more than ten years in the answering?

TWELVE

The opening bars of "Louisiana Saturday Night" filled the car's cabin.

Ava jumped at the chirping tune, pressing her foot harder on the accelerator. The car's tires spun on the loose gravel at the end of the driveway. Her bag of fast-food lunch slid to the floorboard.

The second stanza began to come from the cell's speaker.

Muttering at herself for downloading the song for her ringtone, she dug in her purse for the cell phone.

Where was the silly thing?

Pulling off to the side of the driveway, she located the phone in the side pocket of her purse and flipped it open without even looking at the caller ID. "Hello."

"Ava? This is Paul Fayard, returning your call."

She put a smile into her voice. "Oh. There was no rush. You could've waited until Monday to call back."

"Not a problem. What can I help you with?"

Ava put the car in Park and turned off the ignition. This could take a while, and she didn't want to have the conversation at home where Bosworth or Bea could overhear and report back to her mother. That'd do nothing but start a whole new battle.

"I have a legal question I wanted to ask."

"Shoot."

"Regarding the conclusiveness and legalities of a DNA test."

A long pause ensued.

She tapped her nails against the leather steering wheel cover and stared at her home. The weeping willow in the front yard needed to be trimmed. Spring would sneak up on Loomis soon. Already the breeze carried a hint of budding blooms.

"Is this DNA test a paternity test?" Not surprising he'd figure it out, what with all the gossip going around in Loomis.

"Not exactly."

"Ava, the attorney-client privilege is in force between you and me. You can tell me what's going on."

She let out a sigh. "I know you're aware of Dylan's last words and the implications that came with them. If I agree to a DNA test to run against Sarah Farley, how conclusive would the results be, from a legal standpoint?"

"From Dylan's autopsy samples? About ninety-nine point nine-nine-nine percent conclusive, and the results would stand up in any court."

"Not from Dylan. A DNA sample from me."

"Come again?"

"To show if it's possible that I'm related to Sarah."

Another pause dropped over the connection as heavy as the early morning fog over the bayou.

"Why wouldn't you just use Dylan's DNA samples? The tests are almost one hundred percent accurate, and there's no question of their acceptance in the court systems today. Quite the opposite—they've become the standard in paternity cases."

Here it came, the bombshell. The part where his loyalty would side him with Charla. "Well, Mother refuses to even consider granting permission for the test to be run. She thinks the idea is so outlandish, she won't even discuss it with me anymore."

That was putting her mother's reaction lightly.

"Charla is listed as Dylan's next of kin, and as such, she is the legal representative of any and all of his remains, DNA samples included."

"So I figured." She sighed. "So, matching my DNA against Sarah's—how do those results stand from a legal point of view?"

"They're accepted, of course, but not as conclusive as using a potential parent's. Do you think it would make a difference in Charla's decision if she knew about Dylan coming in and starting the paperwork to petition the court to demand a paternity test on Sarah? I could tell her if you think it'd help."

What? Good thing she wasn't driving because she would've just wrecked her car. "Did he do that?"

"About three weeks ago or thereabouts. I thought you knew."

Apparently, there was a lot about her brother she hadn't been aware of.

"No. I had no idea he'd even thought it possible until his dying words." Now she had to wonder if maybe he'd been clearing his conscience with that cryptic message.

"He came into the office and asked me to draw up a petition to the court to order the test."

"What'd the court determine?"

"We put off filing it then as I advised him that if at all possible, getting the child's mother to agree to the testing would be the best route to go for all involved. We went ahead and drew up the paperwork just to cover all of our bases, but he said he'd meet with Leah and try to get her to agree to the test."

Now she was getting somewhere. "What'd Leah say?"

"I don't know. Dylan never contacted me again about the issue."

Another dead end. Maybe her mother had been right when Leah went missing—she killed her husband and ran. And then came back to kill Dylan. No, that didn't make sense. She would have never left her daughter, not if she killed to protect her.

But at least now Ava knew her brother thought he might have fathered a child. And obviously one he didn't know for sure was his, so she shouldn't feel betrayed by him. Yet she did. He suspected all this and never once confided in her. What kind of sister had she been to him?

"I'm assuming you have a reason for asking?" Mr. Fayard interrupted her thoughts with his question.

"Yes. Sheriff Reed would like the test run."

The lawyer chuckled. "I just bet he would."

For the second time, Ava picked up on Mr. Fayard's apparent dislike of the sheriff. "Why would you say that?"

"Bradford's so close to retirement that he's champing at the bit to get this case closed as soon as possible. No deputy will be willing to run for sheriff if there's a major, multiple-murder case left open."

That could mean the sheriff would use any and all circumstantial evidence he could muster to try and pin the murders on anybody he could.

Such as Max.

"Max, where are you?"

He sighed and put away his papers so his mother wouldn't see. "In the kitchen." Why did she refuse to honor his requests not to just barge in anytime she felt like it? He was so going to get his locks changed and not give her a set of keys this time.

Lenore stepped through the doorway. "It looks much nicer

since the cleaning crew finished up. Were you satisfied with their work, dear?" She bent to plant a kiss on his cheek, and a cloud of Interlude perfume engulfed him.

Standing, he slipped the folder under the phone book on the counter. The less his mother knew about what he was working on, the better. "They were fine."

She glanced into the living area. "Looks like they did an outstanding job to me."

He lifted a single eyebrow. "Kind of sneaky of you to try to slip some religion in on me."

"Oh?" She tilted her head and batted her eyelashes. Her fake ones. "Whatever are you talking about?"

"The blond girl from the church. Don't tell me you didn't specifically hire her to talk to me."

"I hired Janie because she needs the money and Reverend Harmon says she does fine work."

"And you just happened to mention that you keep asking me to come to church and I refuse, right?"

"She asked. I wasn't going to lie." As if his mother was known for her truthfulness and upstanding morals. She glanced out the window, suddenly interested in the breeze tickling the dead magnolia leaves.

"You thought it perfectly okay to encourage her to probe me about why I wasn't coming to church?"

"I had no idea she'd even bring up your lack of spiritual refinement."

Spiritual refinement? Was she serious?

Lenore shrugged. "I just thought she might be a good influence on you."

"That she's cute didn't influence your decision at all?"

"Well, nice looks never hurt anyone, son." She smiled, showing off her puffy, injected-with-something-he-didn't-want-to-know-what lips.

He shook his head. "I've told you not to play matchmaker with me. I can pick my own dates, thank you very much."

Her enhanced lips dropped the smile. "Not very well."

"What's that supposed to mean?" Now she pushed toward crossing the line. Barging into his home aside, his love life was off-limits. He had to take a stand. Now was as good a time as any.

"Just look at your track record, son. Ava Renault. Georgia Duffy." She shook her head and reached for the dish towel folded by the sink. "And now you've been hanging out with Ava once more. It just breaks my heart to see you setting yourself up again." She wiped nonexistent crumbs from the counter.

"This might surprise you, Mom, but I'm a big boy and capable of deciding who interests me."

"But, Max, Av—"

"No. Enough. You don't get to manage my love life."

She didn't argue, just pursed her lips into that famous pout of hers.

"Be careful you don't frown too long, Mom. Makes more wrinkles." He stormed from the kitchen into the living room.

What was his mother's beef with Ava all of a sudden? Sure, she'd hated them dating back in high school and had been livid when he'd moped around like a lovesick puppy after Ava left, but to go so far as to accuse her of framing him for her brother's murder? This had to be more than just a family feud.

Lenore clicked her heels against the floor into the living room. "I'm just trying to look out for you is all." Her voice hinged on whiney.

He spun and faced her. "Why don't you like Ava?"

She blinked rapidly. "Because she broke your heart, of course."

"You didn't like us dating before she went to boarding school. Why's that?"

"She's a Renault, son."

"That's not a good enough excuse anymore. That stupid feud should have ended generations ago. Why keep it flaming?"

"Well, Charl—"

"No. All the two of you have done all my life is be snide toward one another and try to better the other. It's stupid and immature."

Her eyes grew wide. "I did not raise you to speak to your mother like this, Maximilion Arthur Pershing. I won't tolerate it." She spun toward the door, her heels clicking like cicadas on a summer night.

He started to call her back, to apologize, but stopped. It was high time she let him live his own life without her meddling. And if that life included Ava, well, his mother would just have to accept the fact.

A life with Ava…how long had it been since he'd dreamed such a dream? The possibility of it now filled his heart to bursting. Only one thing stood in his way of pursuing her and working out their problems.

Finding out who framed him.

Even the extra spices the cooks, Brandon and Rachel, slipped into the etouffeé didn't excite Ava. Her mind still whirred around who could possibly be framing Max.

"Ms. Ava?"

She jerked her gaze from the notes sitting on the desk before her and looked at Bea. "Yes?"

"Ms. Jocelyn Gold calling for you."

Ava glanced at the phone to her right. Sure enough, the light was lit up. How could she not have heard it ring? "Thank you, Bea."

The maid eased out of the office and closed the door as Ava lifted the handset. "Hey, Jocelyn."

"How are you?" The concern in her friend's voice warmed Ava despite the chilly February evening.

"I'm okay."

"Are you sure? I mean, it's okay to grieve, girl."

Ava smiled into the phone. "I am grieving. I just have a lot of other stuff going on to keep me occupied. Like a certain special someone's wedding."

Jocelyn laughed. "How's that coming along?"

"Good. Everything's right on track. Turned some details over to my assistant, but it looks like everything's good to go." For the first time, she wondered if planning their wedding was the right thing to do. After all, Sam was trying to pin a murder on Max. Of which he was innocent.

"You don't know how much it means to me that you're the one planning my wedding. In spite of everything going on."

No, she had to plan the wedding. For Jocelyn. "I'd have been offended if you hadn't asked."

"Yeah, you would've." Static filled the line. "I'm losing reception, but just wanted to touch base with you. Want to hook up Monday sometime?"

"Sounds like a plan to me. Hey, let's meet for breakfast at Café Au Lait. Bring Sam. I should have some new music samples for y'all to check out."

"We'll be there. Eight-thirty."

The line went dead. Ava hung up the phone and went back to her thoughts. Who killed her brother?

And who was trying to frame Max for the crime?

THIRTEEN

What Charla didn't know wouldn't hurt her.

At least, that's what Ava told herself. She'd spent the majority of the night awake. Praying, thinking, crying, more praying, and had only come to one conclusion—she needed to know the truth, no matter what.

Dressing for church, she swallowed back her apprehension. She'd made her decision and would stick by it, letting the results determine her plan of action. Until then, she had no intention of telling her mother anything. She'd cross that channel when the time came.

Speaking of her mother…would Charla be attending church this morning? She hadn't since Dylan had been killed, but now, with the little bursts of her regular self returning more and more, Ava had to wonder. She set down the tube of lipstick and peered at herself in the mirror. She should find out.

With a sigh, Ava headed downstairs, took a right at the hall and stopped outside the door to her mother's set of suites. Silence reigned on the other side. She rapped her knuckles against the door. "Mother?"

The door swished open, and Bea stood in the doorway with a flourish. "Mrs. Charla's about ready for church. Bosworth's gone to bring the car around."

So her mother felt well enough to attend services. Good. That showed she was definitely on the road to overcoming her grief. Soon, she'd be back in true form.

Which gave Ava little time to figure out who framed Max.

She stiffened her shoulders and entered the room. Charla sat straight in her wheelchair, wearing a linen pantsuit and pearls with her hair perfectly coiffed. She looked more alert and like her old self than she had since the funeral. "You look lovely, Mother."

Charla's gaze slid up and down Ava. "Are you wearing that?"

Ava knew the straight-line dress was very becoming on her and that her mother was most likely just trying to get a rise out of her. Could be that her mother would be back to her regular self sooner rather than later. "I'm delighted you're feeling well enough to attend church this morning."

Her mother gave her a cutting look before glancing at Bea. "How long does it take Bosworth to bring the car around?"

Hair sticking out from her normally neatly smooth bun, Bea ducked her head. "I'll go find out, ma'am."

Bosworth chose that moment to appear in the doorway. "Are you ladies ready?"

"About time." Charla maneuvered her wheelchair around the suite and crossed the threshold.

Ava shot him a sympathetic smile as she followed her mother. If she was lucky, Reverend Harmon would preach on the subject of grace.

The ride to the church was as silent as a crypt. Charla stared out the window, while Ava fidgeted with her conscience. She should tell her mother about Dylan, but she couldn't face an argument on the Lord's day.

Of course, every day was the Lord's.

Yeah, she knew that, but the fight had gone slap out of her.

Too much emotional mess to deal with to add her mother's fits into the mix. At least, not right now. Once she got her DNA test results, then she'd discuss the facts with her mother.

Whether Charla wanted to hear them or not.

Bosworth assisted her mother from the car to the wheelchair, leaving Ava to stumble into the sanctuary alone.

The musical notes of "Amazing Grace" strummed in the background from the speakers. Immediately, a sense of peace floated over Ava, calming her in a way that had escaped her all week.

Thank You, Jesus, for reminding me that I can always rest in You.

She slipped into the pew beside her mother, first row on the right, where the Renaults had sat for nearly all of Ava's life. She glanced across the aisle. The Pershing pew.

Their pew sat empty. Where was Lenore? Max hadn't attended services since Ava returned to Loomis. She'd missed his presence at first, then relished in his absence as she was able to concentrate on the sermon. But now …

Now she wondered what had really caused Max to stop attending church. Was it her return? Or had he totally lost the faith that had once been so strong? Another thing she decided to learn the truth about.

A child's singing behind her brought Ava's gaze around. She sucked in her breath.

Little Sarah Farley held her uncle Clint's hand, singing in an angelic voice the chorus to the old favorite hymn. She stared at Ava with such familiar eyes that Ava's heart raced.

Eyes almost identical to Ava's own.

Before she could even register a cohesive thought, Lenore Pershing pushed past Clint and Sarah. Wearing a white brimmed hat with a tacky blue ribbon, Lenore halted at the end of the pew. Her gaze shot to Charla.

Would she offer some sort of condolence?

Lenore gave a little huff, then scooted into her pew. So much for offering sympathies. Ava had long grown tired of the women's feuding. Undercurrents in the bayou, in her opinion. Why were these mature ladies always acting like children toward one another? It was downright disgraceful.

Clint ushered Sarah into a pew behind Ava. The little girl glanced at Ava and smiled.

Ava's heart melted. If she hadn't already made her decision, that smile would have cinched the deal. She would have the DNA test run as soon as possible.

Just the idea that the precious little girl could be her niece sent thrills through Ava. She winked back before facing the front, her heart filled with anticipation and expectation.

Reverend Harmon took to the pulpit. "Today, our sermon will discuss loving your neighbor, based on the book of Matthew, chapter twenty-two, verse thirty-nine."

Ava smiled. *Thank You, Father.*

Wind danced over the bayou, tickling the Spanish moss draped over the trees. The midday sun shone down from center sky and warmed Loomis.

Max threw another cast into the water, let it sit for a minute then flicked his wrist and began slowly reeling in the bait. A gentle tug pulled against the line. Max jerked the rod, trying to set the hook. He met a brief moment of resistance before the line flew toward him.

Ugh, he'd missed again.

He set down the fishing pole and slipped his chirping cell phone from his pocket. "Hello."

"Hey, Max. It's Ava." As if she had to tell him, from the way his heart reacted to her voice.

"Hi. What's up?"

"I forgot to tell you the flyers for the pageant were delivered Friday afternoon. I ran into MaryBeth at church and she's gathering a group of volunteers to get them posted this afternoon." She paused, as if gathering her thoughts. Or mustering her courage? "I thought maybe you and I could meet and distribute the flyers to the volunteers. Are you busy?"

"Just doing a little fishing off the pier."

She chuckled. "Catching anything?"

"Humble pie."

Her full-bodied laugh filled him with joy. "That bad? You used to be quite the fisherman. Losing your touch?"

All he could remember was how he'd taught her to cast. Wrapping his arms around her to let her feel how to tap the wrist. Standing so close that the smell of her perfume filled his senses and intoxicated him.

"Max?"

"Yeah, I think we should meet." Man, he needed to pay closer attention. Thinking of the past could be dangerous. Especially where Ava was concerned. "When and where?"

"MaryBeth is meeting us at the diner at one. Is that good for you?"

He glanced at his watch. "Yeah. Twenty minutes is fine. I'll just head straight there from here."

"Okay. I'll see you soon."

Snapping the phone shut, Max stared out over the bayou. The water was as smooth as glass. Simply beautiful. He recalled the days when such images of nature made him think of God. Now they didn't.

But today was different. For the first time in many years, he wondered if maybe God had been listening, waiting to answer his prayers. Still, a decade sure seemed like a long time to wait. But what if both he and Ava needed to grow up before their relationship could survive? Had God known this, intervened to give them the opportunity to mature, then orchestrated their reunion?

But what about Micheline's twin, Michael Pershing? God hadn't healed him of the cancer that claimed his cousin and friend's young life. There was no logical reason why his cousin had to die. So much death and ugliness in the world—Max couldn't understand how God could allow such to continue.

Trust in the Lord with all your heart, and lean not on your own understanding.

That was the Scripture the girl had planted in his head. Now he questioned the determinations he'd made.

Max sighed and grabbed his rod and reel along with his tacklebox. Too much to contemplate on a lazy Sunday afternoon. One he'd get to spend with Ava.

After storing his gear in the back of the truck, Max drove all the way across town to Bitsy's Diner. He whipped into the parking lot just as Ava pulled in. His heart did a backflip as she got out and smiled at him over the roof of her car.

He smashed down his schoolboy reaction. "Hiya."

"Hi, yourself." She lifted a large box and shut the car door with her hip.

He moved to take the box from her. "I'd forgotten how many of these we'd ordered."

She smiled, and the world brightened. "You know the mayor—he wants to make sure no one in town will forget to nominate their mother."

Max shook his head and followed her into the diner. "You gonna nominate Charla?" He certainly couldn't see nominating either Charla or Lenore, but Ava's mother was grieving the loss of her son.

Ava snorted in response.

MaryBeth met them just inside the door. "Good, y'all have

the flyers." She turned to face a group of ladies, clapping her hands as she did. "Okay, girls. Y'all have your sections. Put them on poles, storefront windows, and anything else you can stick 'em on. Let's cover Loomis with reminders of the pageant."

Max noticed the blond cleaning girl staring at him from the back of the crowd as MaryBeth handed out stacks of the flyers. Restlessness filled him. He turned to Ava. "I still don't understand why this pageant is such a big deal. Sure, the prizes are okay, but all this hoopla?"

She grinned, sending his stomach back into somersaults. "I think it's mainly to earn bragging rights, if you want to know the truth."

He recalled his younger years, when his mother would hint and hint at him to nominate her. And he had. But Dylan and Ava had nominated Charla as well. One year in particular, he remembered Lenore breaking down in tears in the privacy of her own home, of course, when Charla won the award over her. Could this annual pageant have fed the feud the women loved to engage in?

Satisfied that all the ladies were on track in their mission, MaryBeth turned to him and Ava. "Don't y'all worry a'tall. We'll have those flyers up lickety-split."

"Thank you so much for overseeing the volunteers. We couldn't do it without you, MaryBeth." As usual, Ava's natural grace oozed from every pore.

MaryBeth lapped it up like a coon dog with water after an all-night hunt. A touch of pink even tinged her cheeks. "Just tryin' to help out where I can."

"Well, we really appreciate it." Ava cut her gaze to him. "Don't we, Max?"

"Oh. Most definitely."

MaryBeth preened under his smile. "Oh, how y'all do go on." She nodded at Ava. "I'll make sure everyone completes their sections and collect all the leftover flyers. I can just give 'em to you sometime this week."

"Perfect." Ava shifted her purse strap to her shoulder. "Thanks again, MaryBeth."

"Happy to help."

Slipping her arm through his, Ava led Max from the diner. As soon as they were a few feet from the door, both burst out laughing.

Oh, it felt so good to laugh. And with Ava, too.

"That poor girl is so eager to please." Ava shook her head.

"Overeager, I'd say."

She glanced around, the smile slipping from her face. He followed her line of vision, and his gut tightened. Georgia Duffy stood chatting with one of the volunteers not two hundred yards from him and Ava.

"You know, she has long, red hair," Ava stated.

"Not all that long."

She arched a single brow. "Do we know the exact length of the hair found on Earl and Dylan?"

"I don't. Remember, I didn't even know about the hairs until you told me."

"I don't know the exact length, either." She sighed. "Maybe we should talk to her. She has red hair and had a motive to frame you."

"Georgia? Why would she want to frame me?"

Ava dropped her gaze, as well as her voice. "Maybe she was a bit upset that your relationship ended."

"It wasn't really a relationship, and it was almost six years ago."

Her stare cut him at the knees. "Then what was it?"

Oh, he really didn't want to explain this. Not to Ava. He gave what he hoped looked like a casual shrug. "We just went out a couple of times."

"A couple of times? Funny, that isn't how I remember it."

That she'd noticed surprised him. That a touch of jealousy lurked in her voice filled him with hope. "It wasn't anything serious."

"To you or her?"

"Both." Yet he couldn't help remembering how Georgia had screamed and yelled at him when he told her he didn't want to see her anymore. And he still believed she'd stayed working at Pershing Real Estate in hopes that he'd ask her out again.

"Really?"

He swallowed hard. The hate in Georgia's eyes had made him leery ever since. Now, looking into Ava's earnest gaze, he had to wonder if Georgia had been bitter enough to do something as outlandish as frame him. She could've gotten the medallion in any of the ways Ava had come up with. But why would she kill Dylan? Was it possible Dylan had rejected her as well? The hate in her eyes…well, she might be capable of just about anything.

FOURTEEN

Father, please give me strength. Because Ava sorely needed intervention so she wouldn't give in to the urge to slap the smirk off Georgia's face. Memories of how smug the beauty queen always appeared to Ava stung as she made sure steps down the sidewalk. Like the time Georgia had made homecoming court and Ava hadn't. It'd hurt then, and the memory still hurt today. No matter that it happened almost a decade and a half ago—time *didn't* heal all wounds.

Max cut his gaze to her. "Are you sure you want to do this?"

Ava clenched her jaw and squared her shoulders. "Why ever wouldn't I?"

He gave a curt nod and strode toward the fiery redhead. Ava lengthened her stride to move beside him.

"Hey, Georgia."

The leggy real estate agent stepped away from the volunteer and threw a bright smile at Max. "Hello, sugah. How ya been?" She totally ignored Ava, moving to Max and laying a hand on his forearm.

He shifted away from her touch. "Fine. How're you?"

One of her manicured brows rose. "I'm doing." She finally let her gaze fall to Ava. "Why, hello, Ava. Isn't this a surprise?"

Not hardly. She'd seen them walk out of the diner together

and stand on the sidewalk talking. The years hadn't changed the woman's attitude one iota. "Hey, Georgia."

The tension was as murky as the water in the bayou.

With a toss of her hair over her shoulder, Georgia turned her back to Ava, concentrating on Max. "To what do I owe the honor?"

Ava pivoted to move beside Max. "I'm just curious, Georgia, did you ever date my brother?"

Eyes the color and hardness of emeralds shot to Ava. "Me? Date Dylan?" She laid a dramatic hand across her chest. "I'd never date such a playboy. I only enjoy meaningful relationships, not just a romp in bed."

Yeah, right. Not from what Ava heard. Well, the rumors of Georgia's little indiscretions only started a year or so ago. But still.

Max drew Georgia's attention. "You never even went out with him once?"

"Would you be jealous if I had, sugah?"

"You know, it occurs to me that Dylan never would've gone out with someone like you." Ava clenched and un-clenched her fists.

Georgia just laughed, full and throaty. "As if Dylan was so selective."

Max shot Ava an apologetic smile. "You knew Angelina, didn't you, Georgia?"

A scowl scampered across the redhead's perfectly made up features. "Yeah, I knew her. Silly little thing. Always going on and on about how she'd be Mrs. Dylan Renault before year's end." She shook her head. "Didn't turn out so well for her, now did it?"

"She really believed my brother would marry her?"

"He'd given her more attention than any other woman in town, so why wouldn't she?"

"But he broke it off with her. He told me she'd been getting too serious."

"Yeah. She took it really hard. Was so angry and bitter that he dumped her in such a public place. She was humiliated." Georgia let her scathing glance fall over Ava. "But that's how Dylan was—never cared a bit about anyone else's feelings but his own."

Ava sucked in air and fought to control her breathing.

Max's steady tone cut through the forced civility. "Did you know Leah Farley well?"

"Not really." Georgia smiled at Max as if he were the only person on the planet. "You know me, sugah, I don't have much interest in the mommy world. All Leah ever wanted to talk about was her kid. I was her real estate agent, you know. We were trying to find them a house to get the kid away from the pawnshop. Leah wanted a house with a yard."

Ava nodded. Leah had been a dedicated mother. Which meant that the FBI was probably right—Leah Farley was dead. "I heard she fired you." Ava lifted her chin.

"Wherever did you hear such a silly thing?"

Detecting the hint of unease in Georgia's tone, Ava kept going. "And I heard you'd been flirting with Earl."

A flash of panic burst across Georgia's face. "I don't know where you got your info, sugah, but you've been misinformed."

"Do you happen to remember where you were between ten thirty and eleven thirty on the morning of January 23?"

Placing her bony fists on her hips, Georgia squared off with Ava. "What's with all the questions?" She shifted her stare to Max. "Wanna tell me what's going on here?"

"We're just trying to find some answers," he replied.

Georgia tilted her head. "Because that's the time when Dylan was murdered." She laughed that annoying laugh of hers again. "Oh, this is rich. Y'all think I might've had something to do with the murder?" She snorted, then coughed before glaring at Max. "From what the paper said, you're the prime suspect."

"Someone's framing me."

"Oh, I see. And you think that person is me?" Georgia shook her head and clucked her tongue. "Max, Max, Max…I wasn't as hung up on you as Angelina was on Dylan. We had fun while it lasted, but I never thought of us in the happily ever-after way." She batted her mascara-heavy lashes.

Ava resisted the urge to smack her. "Just answer the question, Georgia. Where were you at the time my brother was shot?"

"Not that it's any of your business, but I'll tell you. Just to show you how incredibly silly y'all are. If you must know, I was in N'Awlins that day judging the Teen Miss Mardi Gras Pageant."

Ava's heart plummeted. Why couldn't Georgia be guilty? That would get Max off the hook. "All day?"

"Yes, sugah, all day. From nine in the morning 'til five-thirty that afternoon. Then we had the crowning ceremony and parade of the court. I didn't get home until after nine, and that's when I heard all the hoopla about your brother." Georgia didn't bother to mask her glare behind polite appearances. "Satisfied?"

As much as she hated to admit it, Georgia had an ironclad alibi. Oh, Ava would still check about the pageant, but it sounded like a Georgia event.

The redhead turned her glare to Max. "I'm shocked that you, sugah, think such of me. I thought you'd know me better."

"I don't know you at all, Georgia." He shook his head. "You've changed over the past few years."

Georgia's gaze danced from Max to Ava. "Ah, I see how it is. You want a second chance with this little heartbreaker." She turned to Ava. "Be my guest, sugah. I have much better things to do with my time." With a little wiggle of her fingers, she turned and sashayed down the sidewalk toward her convertible.

Ava stared after her, fighting the dislike rising in her chest until she felt as if she were suffocating. But Georgia's alibi drummed against her thoughts and brought the original question back into focus. If she didn't frame Max, who did?

That was uncomfortable.

Actually, uncomfortable was too mild of a word. Max watched Ava watch Georgia. Little bursts of unease took a spin around his gut.

Finally, Ava glanced at him. "Guess that rules her out as a suspect of both murderer and framer."

He had to admire her. Even when Georgia had deliberately provoked her and insulted the memory of Dylan, Ava had been nothing less than a true Southern lady. Genteel and regal. His heart pounded. "I guess so."

She let out a sigh. "I suppose it's too much to hope she's lying about being in New Orleans."

The way her mouth turned into a half pout was so cute, Max couldn't help but let out a little chuckle. "I'm thinking she's telling the truth."

"Was she truthful about everything?"

He took her elbow and led her down the sidewalk. "I have no doubt she was at that pageant all day."

"What about what she said in regards to y'all's relationship?"

His stomach tightened. "I told you already, we just went out a couple of times."

"That isn't how she acted."

"She was just trying to get your goat."

"Hmm."

Max walked beside her in silence, letting Ava stew in her

thoughts. Georgia had always rubbed Ava the wrong way. Georgia was a people magnet, while Ava always had been an over-analyzer. One of the things he'd loved most about her and had irritated him the most at the same time. Why should a decade make a difference?

It would never matter that he'd gone out with Georgia only because his mother kept goading him to date. Kept harping on him. So much that he'd finally given in and asked the most available woman handy. Georgia. But back then, she didn't have a reputation. No, she'd earned that only in the last few years, after he'd called off the farce of a relationship.

They'd had a couple of dates—been to the movies and out to eat a couple of times. Maybe they went to a Mardi Gras ball or two. But as soon as she wanted him to come over for supper and get to know her mother, he knew to put the skids on the relationship, but fast. Georgia had been beyond livid, if his memory served him correctly, and it did. But with an airtight alibi…

They reached Ava's Jaguar. He stopped, not knowing what to say or do. She fingered her key ring. "Look, it's none of my business what went on between you and Georgia."

"But there wasn't anything. Nothing more than a couple of dates. And it was so long ago."

She held up her hand. "None of my concern."

"Stop." He grabbed her hand, savoring the soft flesh in his. "Let's stop pretending you and I never had a past."

Jerking her hand free, Ava shook her head. "It was a long time ago, Max."

"Years ago, but I loved you."

Moisture pooled in her eyes. "Let's not do this. Not here. Not now."

He glanced around, spotting the Sunday afternoon walkers who stared, even from across the street. "When, then?"

"Is this really necessary? What's done is done. It's over and in the past."

If only his heart could believe that.

"I think it'd be a good thing to clear the air between us."

"But people …"

"Let's drive out to the pier. Just sit and talk."

Suspicion lurked in her gaze, hurting him. She didn't trust him. Had she ever? "C'mon, Ava. Don't you want to get everything out in the open and deal with it? Haven't we tiptoed around the issue long enough?"

His heartbeat hesitated for as long as it took her to give a brief nod.

"Follow me." He jumped into his truck, backed out, waited for her to get her car out of the parking spot, then led the way to the edge of town.

He still couldn't believe she'd agreed to come. As he pulled into the gravel pit area next to the end of the pier, panic almost engulfed him. What was he going to say? More important, what was she going to say? And how exactly would he react to whatever she shared?

She slammed her car door, walking slowly toward him. Now was the time to find out what had happened all those years ago.

Find out why she'd stopped loving him.

He led the way to the end of the old pier, then plopped down on the rickety old bench he'd often sat upon and prayed for God to bring her back.

Now she was finally here.

Had she lost her mind? Why had she agreed to come talk to Max? Clear the air?—not likely.

Yet she sat on the bench beside him, ignoring that her heart was caught in her throat, and tried to think of what to say.

To his credit, Max remained silent. But just his close proximity stole her thoughts.

Suck it up, Ava. Stop hesitating and just get it all out.

So he could move into hating her.

She twisted to look him in the eye. She owed him that much. "I'm so sorry, Max." She blinked back the tears burning her eyes.

"What happened?" His voice cracked.

And it nearly undid her.

She swallowed, forcing herself to explain. "Mother sent me off to the most horrible boarding school. All girls, mean girls. Snobs." She shuddered as memories held her hostage. "It was nothing like what I knew from Loomis."

Max laid a hand over hers, providing her with immediate comfort. Reassurance she didn't deserve, yet she couldn't bring herself to avoid his touch again. She enjoyed it entirely too much.

"I wrote you every single day, stealing stamps from the teacher's desk and sneaking down to the mailbox to get them out to you."

His eyes widened. "I never received a single letter from you."

She knew that all too well. "I didn't know that at the time. I thought you weren't writing me."

"But I did. Every day. Sometimes, twice a day."

She smiled, his vehement testimony warming her inside. "I know that now, but I didn't then. All I could think was that you'd moved on. Forgotten me."

"No." He shook his head and squeezed her hand.

Ava inhaled deeply, dreading going any further. But she had to. Max waited for the long-deserved truth. "I didn't know Mother had made arrangements to have my incoming mail tossed and someone to follow me and destroy any correspondence I had written you."

"She destroyed our letters?"

"And denied my phone access except to call home. Even sneaking and using someone else's phone code had your number blocked."

Disgust seeped into his features. Ah, she knew it well.

"But at the time, I didn't know this. All I knew was that you didn't write and didn't call." She swallowed, the lump in her throat nearly choking her. "I cried a lot that year. My senior year, ruined. All because of my mother."

"Oh, Ava." He leaned close, planting a feathery kiss against her temples.

She wanted nothing more than to lean against him, let him comfort and reassure her. But she couldn't. She didn't deserve that. Ava shrugged from his embrace. "When I finally graduated, I learned Mother had already made arrangements for me to return to Loomis and attend the university here." She smiled. "I was excited. I was coming home. I was coming back to you."

"But I had already left for LSU."

"Mother knew that and didn't tell me. Let me believe you were still in town." The enormity of her mother's invasion in her life slammed against her once more. She pushed down the now-familiar resentment and continued.

"I came back and learned you'd gone. I was beyond distraught. Mother wouldn't even allow me to wallow. No, I had to keep my grades up, keep being the perfect daughter. She even went so far as to tell me what I should become."

"I wondered why you became a wedding planner."

"That was why. At that point, I was so hurt and felt so betrayed, I didn't even care. I let her make all those important decisions."

"Why?" He ran a thumb under her chin.

Chills tickled her skin. "Because I'd been told you were very involved with someone else at college, and if I'd ever cared about you, I should just let you go."

"Your mother told you that?" His eyes were so filled with concern, yet anger.

Oh, she hated to tell him. But tell him she must.

"No. Your mother did."

FIFTEEN

"My mother did what?" Max's mind couldn't quite wrap around what Ava had just told him. He'd expected lies and manipulation from Charla, but from his own mother? How conniving of her. Anger seeped into his veins.

"I was desperate. I visited your mother, hoping she'd give me your address or number, anything."

"You went to see her?" Ava had to have been at wits' end to risk having Charla find her at the condo. And then to have his mother lie.

"Yes. She looked me square in the eye and told me you'd fallen in love with some girl at college and if I'd ever cared anything about you, I'd not contact you and just move on with my life." Ava's eyes shimmered with moisture. "She basically told me to forget you and what we had together."

Anger held his heart in its tight fist. "And you believed her?"

"Why wouldn't I, Max? Unlike my mother, she'd never shown any indication that she had a problem with you and me being together."

Oh, he should've told her the truth—how much his mother hated them dating. He hadn't because he didn't want to hurt her feelings. And he'd known how much grief Charla had laid on her. "She did. And I should've told you, but I didn't want to hurt you."

Big tears swam in the pools of her hypnotic green eyes. The Renault eyes. How many nights had he lain awake, haunted by their image?

"I should've figured it out. But I was so hurt, felt so betrayed…well, I didn't think clearly."

"Oh, Ava." He wrapped an arm around her shoulders, drawing her against him. "I'm so sorry."

She hugged him for a long second, then moved away. "At first, I just wallowed in misery. Then, I went a little crazy."

"Crazy, how?"

"I joined a sorority in college. Started hanging around some new people to town." She ducked her head, her strawberry hair shining in the sun. "Dated some boys I knew my mother wouldn't approve of." She let out a shuddering sigh. "I think I did that just to annoy her. I didn't care about them. Not a single one."

Something strange twisted in his gut as trepidation spread in his chest. "And?" His heart rumbled as loud as rolling thunder.

"And I really strayed as far away from my faith as you can ever imagine." Big tears leaked from her eyes.

"How so?" His stomach wound in such a tight knot, he didn't think he'd ever get it untangled. It was one thing to have been aching to have her back—it was another thing entirely to hear the pain their mothers had caused her.

"I began to drink a little. Then, a lot. Smoke. Try things I never should have."

"What are you telling me, Ava?"

Her tears fell freely. "I did so much I'm not proud of, Max. I did things just to make myself feel numb, anything to stop feeling the pain and betrayal." She sobbed, hanging her head and covering her face with her hands.

He wanted to comfort her, wanted to tell her it was okay, but he couldn't lift his arm. Couldn't open his mouth and speak. Couldn't even think straight. Shock held him in check. Ava, drinking and smoking? The girl he'd known nearly had an asthma attack when walking past smokers.

His heart pounded so hard that his chest hurt. What drugs had she done? What had she done under their influence?

Her sobs subsided and she lifted her gaze to his face. He struggled to mask his shock from her probing gaze, knowing she was looking for reassurance and understanding.

She sniffed. "About then, Daddy came to see me, sat me down and really talked to me. Took me to see Reverend Harmon." She smiled through tears. "I rededicated my life to Jesus and got myself straightened out."

"How?" He hated that he couldn't give more than a noncommittal reply, but his heart was having a hard time. Guilt nearly strangled him. If only he'd been there. If only he'd known.

"Finished college magna cum laude. Set up a local business right here in Loomis, to stay close to the church and Daddy. And Dylan. Fought to keep my life on track."

"Then why…" Max struggled with his next question, suspecting the answer but wanting to hear it from her. "Then why, when I returned from college, did you avoid me like the plague? You didn't think I'd notice you crossing the street to avoid passing me? Did you think that wouldn't hurt my feelings?"

Oh, it had almost ripped his heart right out of his chest.

"For one, Mother told me that Pershing Land Developing had lured clients away from the Renault Corporation. Stole investments from Dylan. And that you were the one calling the shots, even from Baton Rouge."

"And you believed such nonsense?"

She met his stare head-on. "I believed your mother."

Touché. Both women were liars with total disregard for their children's happiness.

"And you have to remember, I thought you'd been involved with someone in college, and I was upset." Her cheeks turned a slight shade of pink. "I wasn't exactly proud of my past, Max. I wasn't as pure as the driven snow, and that made it hard to face you."

Max ran his hands over his face. He wanted to shake her mother. His mother.

He wanted to turn back time.

Could Max ever get over what she'd done? What she'd believed about him? Her rebellion?

The earthy smell of bayou drifted on the cool breeze circling the pier. Ava pulled her sweater tighter around her shoulders. She wanted nothing more than to crawl into a hole and never come out. But she'd come this far. She hauled in a deep breath. "It was only months after you returned that I found out the truth. Surprisingly, from Dylan."

"I don't follow."

"Angelina told Dylan that Georgia told her you were never involved with anyone in college. Period." Ava failed to mention how much her heart had pounded when her brother had told her. Hope flared. But just as quickly, she remembered her own past. The balloon of hope had burst.

Max stared at her, his expression frozen in an undetectable mask. "I didn't even date in college." His voice was thready, gravely.

"I shouldn't have believed your mother, Max. What I should have done was get in my car and drive to Baton Rouge and hunt you down on campus to talk to you."

"Why didn't you?"

Good question. One she'd asked herself many times over the last several years. "Maybe I just didn't have enough faith in us." Her heart ached in an old, familiar way.

He ran a hand over his hair. How she longed to run her fingers through the waves. She curled her hands into fists.

An egret swooped low over the water, scooped up a fish, then took flight again. Why couldn't she just fly off as well? Far away from Loomis. From Max. From the truth of their tangled pasts filled with lying mothers and regret.

Max let out a long breath. "I'm furious at my mother, but, Ava, you should've sought me out."

The first wisps of anger smoked across her heart. "You knew I was back in Loomis. Why didn't you seek *me* out?"

Max opened his mouth, hesitated, then snapped it shut.

"Not so easy, right?"

"No. Nothing about this is easy." Again, he raked his hands over his sculpted face.

She wiped the sweat from her palms across her jeans. "So, now you know."

Yes, he finally knew the truth. Honestly, the truth wasn't as bad as he'd expected. At least, not on Ava's part. His mother was a totally different story. In his worst-nightmare scenario, Ava had just fallen out of love with him. But now…well, he could understand why she'd avoided him. He didn't agree with her logic, but he could understand it.

"And it's in the past, right?" Her eyes held so much hope in their intensity.

"Yes. It's in the past." He took her hand in his, rubbing his thumb over her knuckles.

"Then can I ask you one last thing, and we can just put the past behind us?"

"Sure." But his heart quickened.

"What happened to your faith, Max?" She pivoted slightly to stare him in the eye. "You were once so strong for Jesus, sharing your testimony, a walking witness for the gospel. But now, I haven't seen you in church since I got back to Loomis. What happened?"

He'd rather have to discuss a past drug use than explain how he felt. Especially to Ava. Letting go of her hand, he rested his elbows on his knees, hunching against the cooler breeze coming off the bayou.

She laid a hand on his shoulder. Warm. Comforting. Reassuring. How many times had he ached for that touch? And God had said no.

"It's hard to explain, Ava."

"Try." She leaned closer to him, not quite touching him, but her scent and essence surrounding him.

"I guess I used to think He really cared about our day-to-day problems down here on earth. That He listened to our prayers and answered. That He was our strength."

"But you don't anymore?" Her voice cracking almost killed him.

"No. Not like I did. I felt like a hypocrite for believing He'd always be there for me." Learning that He wasn't had broken Max's heart more than Ava leaving.

"Oh, Max. You know better."

He twisted to face her. "Do I? How's that? I prayed nightly for you to come back to me. Yet, here it is, years and years later, and we're just now talking."

"But I am here now. So are you." She stood, the wind softly lifting her golden hair. "I don't know why all things happen, I just know that God has a plan for it all. Even if we never understand it this side of heaven." Her footfalls thumped against the weathered wood of the pier as she paced. "Maybe we were too young, too delusional about the real world for it to have worked."

"You really believe that?" Their love had been strong, not some infatuation.

She stopped in front of him, staring down at him with tears in her eyes. "I don't know, Max. Maybe God needed me to walk on the wild side a bit so that when I came back to Him, I was wiser, more mature, and had learned my lesson."

"Not to do drugs?"

Her expression fell to one of despair. "No, not to wander from His will for me. It was truly the loneliest time of my life. Even worse than thinking you'd found someone else."

Words wouldn't form in his mouth.

She plopped back on the bench beside him. "Don't you think it's foolish to blame God for what our mothers did to us? They're the ones who lied and broke our trust."

"Then how can you continue to live with her?" At this moment, he was seriously considering moving out of Pershing Plaza, just to get away from his mother's interference. Especially now that he knew the truth.

"Because after the wreck and Daddy dying, her being in a wheelchair...well, I just felt sorry for her. She needed me." Tears squeezed out the edges of her eyes and made tracks down her cheeks. "For the first time in my life, my mother needed me. I felt like I mattered."

He wrapped an arm around her shoulders, pulling her tight against him as he fought his very, very strong dislike of Charla Renault. "You've always mattered to me, Ava. A lot."

Moving on instinct—or was it memory?—he leaned forward and brushed his lips over each of her eyelids. Then he planted soft kisses down the bridge of her nose to the tip. His heart swelled in his chest until it felt like he would explode. Slowly, he lowered his mouth to hers.

It was like old times, but different. Slower. More cautious. Yet full of the emotions he'd never forgotten. He ended the kiss and rested his forehead against hers, putting them eye to eye.

"An awful lot."

SIXTEEN

Ava's first thought the next morning, as the sun filtered in through the windows, was of Max. He'd kissed her, bringing every feeling she thought she'd buried back to the surface. And she'd learned he'd totally lost his faith. Now she didn't know what to feel.

On one hand, she could easily let herself fall right back in love with Max Pershing, and if she'd been reading the signals from him right, they could have a second chance at their happily ever after. But when she'd rededicated her life to Christ, she'd vowed to not even date someone who didn't share her faith. Oh, how tangled her life had become.

God, I could sure use a little guidance in everything down here.

She ran a finger over her bottom lip absentmindedly. Max had hijacked her dreams last night, leaving her fitful and anything but rested this morning. She kicked back the covers and padded to the bathroom. No time to get into an emotional tornado this morning. She had places to go, things to do. After she met with Jocelyn and Sam at the hotel's coffee and beignets shop, she'd run into the Renault Corporation and grab the department reports.

The shower she raced through didn't wash away the memory

of Max's kiss. Frustration mounting over her conflicting emotions, Ava dressed in a slick business suit, grabbed her planner and stomped down the stairs and out the front door. Good thing she'd parked her car in the circle instead of the garage.

She breezed into Café Au Lait, arriving at eight-thirty on the dot. The enticing aroma of full-flavored coffee and delectable beignets hovered in the air. Jocelyn stood and waved her over to the window table where she and Sam sat. As Ava wove through the breakfast crowd, a jolt of something unfamiliar hit her. Sam and Jocelyn looked so happy, so in love, so *together*. Her own single status ached within her.

Drat Max for kissing her and bringing all these old feelings up.

Jocelyn hugged her before she sat. "What's wrong?"

"Nothing. Just a lot on my mind." Ava slipped out of her suit jacket and hung it on the back of the chair. She wondered why Jocelyn had to fall in love with the man trying to pin a murder on Max.

"Are you sure?" Jocelyn's eyes were filled with kindness, and for a moment, Ava was sorely tempted to just tell her friend everything.

But this was about Jocelyn's wedding. Her happiness. Her future. Ava smiled. "I'm fine. Early morning."

The wedding plans were finalized as they drank the strong, chicory coffee and ate the donut concoction made famous in New Orleans. Ava made notes of things to have Cathy take care of for her, then assured Jocelyn that her wedding would be beautiful and special. Just like Jocelyn herself. Ava had just slipped her planner into her purse and prepared to say goodbye when MaryBeth entered the hotel's café and rushed to their table.

"They're gone!" The young woman looked as if she'd just wrestled a catfish from a trotline.

Ava stood. "Calm down, MaryBeth. Have a seat."

"I can't. I have to find the sheriff. They're all gone."

Jocelyn shot to her feet as well and placed a hand on MaryBeth's shoulder. "What's gone, honey?"

"The flyers. From all over town. All of them are gone."

"What flyers?" Sam remained sitting, but he missed nothing.

MaryBeth tossed him an exasperated glare. "For the Mother of the Year pageant. We just hung them yesterday afternoon. Now, every single one of them is gone. Just, poof, gone."

"I'm sure there's a simple explanation. It'll be okay." Jocelyn patted MaryBeth.

"There were more than one hundred of them. They couldn't have just disappeared." MaryBeth wrung her hands as she stared out the front window. "I need to go talk to the sheriff first thing."

Before Ava or Jocelyn could say a word, MaryBeth rushed out of the café and headed down the street.

"That is odd," Ava mumbled.

Sam tossed bills onto the table and stood. "That some flyers are missing? Surely stuff like this happens all the time, even in Loomis."

"There were actually two hundred and fifty of them." Ava lifted her purse.

Jocelyn pushed in her chair. "Maybe MaryBeth just noticed some missing. They all can't be gone. Not that many."

Ava led the way a block down where MaryBeth had the sheriff cornered just outside the sheriff's station. Her voice carried on the morning wind. "And now every slap one of them is gone, Sheriff. Just disappeared."

"I'll look into it, MaryBeth."

"Do you need to take my statement or something?"

"Not just yet. Let me see what I can find out."

MaryBeth turned to spot Ava, Jocelyn and Sam. She focused on Ava. "We saved the file on my jump drive, so I'll just take that right over to the printer shop and get some more made. Don't you worry about a thing. We'll have those flyers replaced before the sun sets."

"It's okay." But Ava's words were useless as MaryBeth rushed toward her car.

The sheriff shook his head. "With everything going on in town, she's worried about missing pieces of paper?"

A loud clap from the alley off Main Street caused all three to jump. The lid of a trash can rolled onto the sidewalk and settled with a racket.

Chuck Peters, clearly inebriated even though it was barely midmorning, ambled out of the dark alley. He squinted against the early sun and leaned against the brick wall.

"Hey, Chuck. You see people running around town last night tearing down papers?" Sheriff Reed hollered out.

The town drunk wobbled but slowly focused on them. His eyes widened when the sheriff's uniform registered with him. "I didn't see nothing. You can't make me say I saw something!" He swaggered back into the alley.

"Hey, come back here." Sam took a step to follow Chuck.

The sheriff grabbed Sam's arm. "Don't waste your time. That guy's been a drunk for the last two decades. He's as loony as they come." He let his hand drop when he caught Sam's glare. "I'll look into the missing flyers when we get time."

Ava wondered. Chuck might be drunk most of the time, but he seemed pretty smart to her when he was sober.

"Did y'all need to see me about anything, or can I go get my cup of coffee?" Sheriff Reed scowled at them.

"Actually, I do need a minute of your time." Ava swallowed, hoping he didn't ask her to explain out here in the middle of the street. She knew Jocelyn had worked with little Sarah, and there was no sense stirring up anything until they knew if Dylan was the child's father.

A sheriff's cruiser skidded to a stop curbside. Deputy Bertrand stuck his head out the window. "We got the warrant to impound the car. Want to deliver it? The tow truck's already on the way."

Sheriff Reed darted his gaze from Ava to Deputy Bertrand, as if trying to decide what he should do. Sam stepped in. "I'll go with your deputy and serve the warrant and impound the car. You take care of Ms. Renault's issue."

The sheriff didn't have time to respond before Sam kissed Jocelyn's temple and jumped into the car with Deputy Bertrand.

Ava gave her friend a sideways hug. "I'll call you later." Then she looked at the sheriff. "Shall we?"

He allowed her to enter the station before him, his boots grazing the dirty tile behind her. The stench of burned coffee permeated the room. He directed her to his office and closed the door behind them. After dropping into the wooden chair behind the desk, the sheriff leaned back on two legs. The chair groaned in protest. "Have a seat."

"I'd prefer to stand. This will only take a minute."

"Suit yourself. What can I do for you?"

"It's about the DNA test."

"Charla agreed?" All four legs of the chair hit the floor with a thump.

"Not exactly. But I've done some research and a DNA test on me is acceptable in court to prove if someone is a relative or not."

"But not as reliable."

"Almost as much, but not quite."

The sheriff stood. "I appreciate you coming by and all, Ava, and agreeing to having a test run on you, but right now, it's not needed."

Her pulse skipped. "I don't understand. Why not?"

"Clint Herald, Sarah's uncle, refuses to allow the test to be run on Sarah. Says he won't consent as her temporary guardian as he thinks it's unethical to do so without his sister's consent.

And since Leah's still missing and hasn't been declared legally dead, we can't do anything."

"But doesn't he want to know? Especially if Leah never comes back? Doesn't he want to know if I'm Sarah's aunt? If she has other relatives to help in raising her?"

"Can't say. All I know is he refuses and says that shrink friend of yours agrees with him." Sheriff Reed reached for the door. "Maybe you should argue your case to her."

Or maybe she should just go bury her head and pretend this would all be over and done with by morning.

Yeah, and gators would sprout wings and fly, too.

Bam! Bam! Bam!

Max rushed to the door. He was running late enough as it was, having overslept because he'd tossed and turned all night, unable to get Ava—or their kiss—out of his mind.

He jerked open the door, ready to give an earful to the person banging before ten. Words caught in his throat as he spied Deputy Bertrand and FBI agent Sam Pierce lurking on his doorstep. "To what do I owe the honor? Another attempt at helping me redecorate my place?"

Sam handed him a folded piece of paper. "Here's a warrant to impound your car."

"For what?" Max's hands trembled as he unfolded and read the writ of warrant.

"Further evidence that will put you at the scene of Dylan Renault's murder." The FBI agent wore his smirk as proudly as his badge.

"That'll be hard to do since I'm not the one who killed him."

"Oh, you're good, I'll give you that." Sam nodded as a tow truck backed up to the Benz and lowered the towing chain. "I suggest you call your lawyer, Pershing."

Max clenched his jaw. "Are we done?"

Sam grinned. "For now." He turned and headed toward the tow truck.

Wanting nothing more than to punch the agent square in the kisser but knowing it wouldn't be the smartest move to make, Max went into the kitchen and called Lyle Tanner's office. Mr. Tanner's secretary took the message, then Max scanned the warrant.

Blah, blah, blah…cast of tires to be made to comparison test against the tracks made at the scene of the crime…blah, blah, blah…eyewitness identified car at the scene.

Whoa! Stop everything. An eyewitness? Since when? He hadn't heard anything about an eyewitness. Were they just messing with him? But, no, a judge had signed the warrant. Great heavenly day, what was going on?

He grabbed his keys from the foyer table and nearly got nailed by the front door flying open.

"Why is that silly deputy having your car towed?" Lenore stood in the doorway, eyes blazing.

So not the person he wanted to see right now. Not after learning what she'd done to Ava. And him.

Max sighed and pocketed his keys. He didn't want to get into the discussion of her lying to Ava. Not now. Not when he was already past late for work. "They're impounding it."

"Whatever for?"

"They say it will prove I was at the scene of Dylan's murder."

"Oh, that's ludicrous. This is getting ridiculous. I'm calling Bradford." Lenore took two steps toward the kitchen.

Max stopped her. "Mom, did you see the sheriff out there? This is all the doing of that FBI agent."

The fight left his mother. She sagged against the doorway. "This can't be happening. You didn't do anything."

While still spitting mad at his mother, he couldn't ignore what all of this was doing to her. He wrapped his arm around her shoulders and gave her a tight squeeze. "It's going to be okay. I already called Mr. Tanner and he'll take care of this. We just have to believe the truth will all come out." But he didn't mention what his lawyer had told him about innocent people being convicted.

His mother's face turned an even whiter shade of pale. "I just have to do something. They can't keep thinking you're a murderer."

He planted a kiss on the crown of her head. "It'll be fine. Don't worry." With a slight shift, he moved an arm's length away. "I'm going to work. I'll talk to you tonight."

And wouldn't that be an interesting conversation?

Ava answered her cell phone as she paced the elevator taking her to Dylan's office. Correction, *her* office.

"You are not going to believe this." Max's voice was roughened with stress.

She shook her head to focus, opened the office and flipped on the light. "What now?"

"They just impounded my car."

"You're kidding." She sank into the leather chair behind the desk. "Why?"

"I wish I were. They say they'll recover evidence that will put me at the scene of Dylan's murder."

They were wrong. Just like they'd been wrong about Dylan killing Angelina. Max was being framed. She *knew* that. Her heart wouldn't betray her so badly. "What kind of evidence?"

"According to the warrant, to match my tires against tracks left at the scene. And get this, an eyewitness identified my car as being there."

"What eyewitness?" Her heart raced as adrenaline pushed through her veins.

"I don't know. I was hoping maybe you'd heard something."

"No. But I'll find out, you can bet on that." Why hadn't they been told there was an eyewitness? What were these people doing?

"I called my lawyer and left a message." Fear seeped over the connection. "I know I wasn't there, Ava, but somebody's setting me up."

"I wonder if this new eyewitness is the one framing you." But who?

"It could be the murderer. Do you remember what the sheriff said when he came to tell you about Dylan?"

Ava shook her head reflexively, even though Max couldn't see her over the phone. "I wasn't home. I'd been finishing up a wedding in Covington and was driving back when Bosworth called me and told me the sheriff had been by and that Dylan was dead and Mother wasn't taking the news well."

"Your mother never said?"

"My mother hasn't said much of anything to me since that night. And certainly nothing about how she found out."

"These details might be important, Ava. Think. In every conversation you've had with the sheriff and deputies, have they ever mentioned an eyewitness?"

She closed her mind, replaying all the painful exchanges. "No, not once that I remember. And I think I would have remembered something so important."

"I don't know, but they sure aren't going to tell me anything."

No, they wouldn't. Every little clue she'd gotten from the sheriff she'd had to drag out of him. She squared her shoulders and lifted her purse.

"But they'll tell me, or they'll wish they had."

SEVENTEEN

What could be taking the sheriff so long?

Ava tapped the toe of her designer pump on the dirty floor. It reeked inside the poorly ventilated station. She'd already been waiting a good fifteen minutes to see Sheriff Reed. What, had he snuck out for an early lunch? The man did like to eat.

"Ms. Renault." He stood behind the cracked Formica counter. "Can I help you with something?" So formal.

"As a matter of fact, you can. I need to know some details about my brother's case."

He shifted his weight from one foot to the next, glancing at the clock over her head. Probably trying to figure out if he could get rid of her before the noon hour. He sighed and opened the swinging door. "Come on back."

His office was as dirty and stinky as before. He waved her to a chair, which she declined as gracefully as she could. No way was she sitting in that thing. "What can I help you with?"

"I'm curious, Sheriff, how did y'all discover Dylan's body? And happen to arrive on the scene before he died?"

"Why are you asking this now?"

There he went again, answering a question with a question. "Just call me curious. I never heard it straight from the horse's mouth, so to speak."

"We already went over this with your mother."

"I wasn't there. Humor me, please." She crossed her arms over her chest. Her nails dug into her forearms.

"We received a tip about hearing a gunshot, then finding the body."

"A tip?"

"A phone call."

"From whom?"

He narrowed his eyes. "I'm not at liberty to discuss certain aspects of the case with you. The person prefers to remain anonymous."

Sure he did. If there was even such a person, why wasn't he the prime suspect? "Have you questioned this person about why they were there? Renault Hall is private property. And let's admit it, Sheriff, it's a little out of the way of most people's driving routes. Sounds a little fishy to me."

"We checked out the witness. He's not the murderer."

"You're sure? Did he have an alibi? I mean, being there at the time of the shooting is very suspect to me."

"We're positive."

She tapped her toe again. "Then what was he doing out there?"

"He heard the gunshot—the reverberations carry far over the bayou, ya know—and went to check it out. He found your brother and went to the closest pay phone, at the grocery store on the corner of Church Street."

"Why didn't he come to our house? I mean, it was Dylan who was shot. It's much closer than going two blocks to use a pay phone. Someone's always home at the house."

"I can't say why he didn't."

"So y'all arrived soon after he called?"

A hint of red dotted the sheriff's cheeks. "Within an hour."

"An hour?!" Indignation fused with rage and stiffened her

spine. "Let me get this straight—it took y'all an *hour* to get to the scene? You're less than four blocks away, for pity's sakes. What took you so long?"

The red spread all the way to the tips of his ears. "Well, we considered it might be a prank phone call, so we didn't respond until he called back a second time."

"Wait a minute. He had to call back a second time?" This was getting worse by the minute. Disregarding the possibilities of germs waiting to jump on her, she sank to the chair. Her legs wouldn't support her any longer. "A prank? Who jokes about someone getting shot? Isn't it your job to follow up on all such reports? This is outrageous!" And might put the department at a huge risk of being sued. She'd have to call Mr. Fayard about this new information.

"Let's just say we knew who the caller was, and in the past he hasn't been the most accurate for reporting information."

"Yet, you'll accept his innocence."

"He's unreliable, yes. A murderer, no."

"So you let my brother lie out there dying for an hour? Because you were too lazy to check?" She couldn't believe this. It was shameful. Maybe Dylan could've been saved if they'd acted quicker.

As if reading her mind, the sheriff shifted in his chair. "Dylan had no chance of survival, Ava. I know that's hard to hear, but you can ask the paramedics and doctors. The location of the bullet made the shot fatal. No matter if he'd been shot in an operating room."

"Covered your bases there, Sheriff? This is appalling." She shook her head as another thought slammed against her mind. "But had you gotten there earlier, maybe you could have gotten more out of Dylan than just two words. Have you thought of that?"

"What's done is done. We can't play what-ifs."

Of course they couldn't. Not since they'd messed up so

royally. "And you think this unreliable witness is telling the truth about not being involved? How can you even remotely justify that logic?"

"Why would he call in—twice—if he was involved? He doesn't have a mean bone in his body. Besides, this guy doesn't like drawing police attention, I assure you."

"Yet, he called it in. He didn't walk away."

Sheriff Reed gave a half shrug. "Guess he had a moment of conscience."

"But you believe him?"

"Yes."

She shoved to her feet. "Then why won't you believe Max Pershing?"

"Because there's physical evidence that links him to the crime."

"Obviously this guy was at the scene, too."

Sheriff Reed let out a heavy sigh. "Trust me, Ava, I'd like to close this case, but there's no way this witness is involved. No way."

"Well, there's physical evidence that links Dylan's murder to Earl's, but I don't see you following up on that connection."

"Actually, we are. And we've learned Max had an altercation just before Christmas with Earl. Right in the middle of Loomis Park."

Her limbs trembled. She leaned against the doorframe. "But that's just rumor, Sheriff. You know how the people in this town love to gossip."

He stood facing her. "Maybe so, but that eyewitness says he saw a red car, a convertible, speed away from Renault Hall after your brother was shot."

Ava's heart hiccupped. "But you said he's unreliable."

"Which is why we're checking out Max's car right now."

Max's red Mercedes-Benz.

Which had had the medallion in the console that'd been found in Dylan's pocket.

Great. Just great. Two more clients backed out of real estate deals. Made the grand total of eight lost clients since the weekend newspaper ran the article on him being implicated in Dylan's murder.

Max slammed the file drawer shut, wishing he could slam that FBI agent's head instead. How could he honestly think Max would shoot Dylan? Fishing. That's what all this was. They had nothing to go on so they were tossing out nets, trying to catch something.

Too bad that something had snagged him.

His intercom buzzed and Patsy's cheerful voice filled his dark office. "Ava Renault on line one for you, boss."

He didn't even bother to thank his secretary, just pressed the button and lifted the phone. "Ava." Maybe she had good news. Or anything but bad.

"I'm leaving the sheriff's station. Can you meet me for lunch now?"

"Bitsy's?"

"No. Too busy. How about Super Burger?"

It must be serious if she wanted to meet for a hamburger. Even as a teenager, Ava hadn't been wild about fast food. "Sure. I'll leave right now."

He told Patsy he would be out for lunch, then headed to the parking lot. Ava's voice had sounded stressed. What now?

Whipping onto Church Street, he spied the agent's car parked in front of the sheriff's station. They were probably going over his car with a fine-tooth comb. Waste of their time and energy. Time they could be spending trying to find the real killer.

One block up, he passed the pawnshop where Leah and Earl Farley had lived directly above. A piece of yellow crime-scene tape fluttered from an upstairs window. He ignored the arguments raging in his mind and turned into the parking lot of the burger joint. Ava's Jaguar sat parked beside a clunker of a Chevy.

She was easy to spot as soon as he entered through the glass door with a bell hanging above. A vision among the ordinary. He twisted and turned through the crowded burger dive that was already packed with early lunchers. The cloud of grease and pepper aroma hung about eye level. The air reeked with the smell of pungent onions. He dropped into the vinyl booth seat across from her.

"I ordered you a burger with everything except onions, and a tea." She smiled at him and smoothed the paper napkin.

She still remembered how he liked his burger. They belonged together, on so many levels. He knew they did. If only they could figure out who was framing him for murdering her brother. The underlying tension between them wouldn't go away until they knew.

"Thanks. I appreciate it."

The waitress appeared with their iced teas, set them on the table along with lemon wedges and rushed off.

"You having a burger, too?" He winked, already knowing the answer.

"Um. No. I'm having the house salad."

"I figured." He squeezed the lemon over his tea, then dropped the wedge into the glass. "So, what'd you find out?"

"Seems there's an eyewitness of sorts," she began, and then filled him in on all she'd learned from Sheriff Reed.

The waitress returned and plopped their plates down in front of them. Never before had a burger and fries looked so unappealing. Just the greasy aroma threatened to send him running outside.

"And that's why they impounded your car." She stared at him for a long moment, her expression unreadable.

When he said nothing, she clasped her hands over her salad. "I'm going to bless the food."

He ducked his head, numbly doing as instructed.

"Father God, we thank You for the many blessings You've bestowed upon us. Sometimes, in situations such as what we're going through now, it's hard for us to understand Your will. But, Father, we trust in You with all our hearts, and lean not on our own understanding. Bless this food for the nourishment of our bodies and our bodies to Your service. Amen."

Words failed him. She'd prayed the exact same Scripture that girl had quoted to him. Was God trying to get his attention?

Ava applied a thick layer of pepper over her salad before she lifted her fork and met his gaze. "I think their witness is Chuck Peters."

"Why would you say that?"

"Who else could it be? He fits everything the sheriff told me. Unreliable. Avoids the police. Wouldn't hurt anyone. They wouldn't immediately follow up on anything he reported. He's the logical explanation."

"Makes sense." But that still didn't explain how Chuck saw the Benz there. He brought the question before Ava.

She took another bite of her salad and chewed slowly. "It's very likely he's mistaken."

"I'd think finding Dylan shot and dying would be enough to sober him even if he was three sheets to the wind."

"True." She wiped her mouth with the paper napkin. "Who else has a red convertible?"

"Georgia."

"And she was in New Orleans, or so she says." She yanked her little leather appointment book from her purse and jotted down a note. "I forgot to call and verify she was at the pageant. I'll do that this afternoon."

He took the first bite of his burger, hoping it didn't come right back up, and glanced at some of the papers from Ava's book.

He nearly choked.

Max swallowed without finishing chewing. He sputtered and coughed. Drank half a glass of iced tea. Sucked in air.

"Are you okay?"

He nodded despite his watering eyes. When he finally caught his breath, he tapped the edge of one of the papers. "What's this?"

She glanced over her handwritten notes before staring at him with confusion circling her expression. "Just some wedding business stuff. Why?"

"Whose wedding?"

"My friend's. Jocelyn Gold."

"Who's she marrying?" He wadded his napkin into his fist.

"Sam." Her face took on a pained look. "Oh."

"How can you plan the wedding of the man who's doing his best to convict me of a murder I didn't commit?" How could she do this to him? He couldn't even describe how he felt, just that a part of him went numb. Knowing how FBI Agent Sam Pierce was fighting to put Max behind bars, Ava would still plan his wedding?

She set down her fork and tossed the crumpled napkin into the bowl. "Jocelyn's one of my dearest friends."

"And Sam Pierce is my mortal enemy."

"He's just doing his job, Max."

"Like Bradford Reed did when he hounded Dylan about Angelina's murder?"

Her eyes told him he'd hit his target. "I'm so sorry, Max."

"Then stop planning his wedding. Let him figure out how to do that." He snorted. "Maybe then he'll leave me alone."

"I can't back out on Jocelyn. Not now."

Again, he was second fiddle to Ava.

"Then I guess that says it all." He stood, threw a twenty on the table and strode out of Super Burger.

"Max, wait." Ava's voice trailed behind him.

He didn't stop. Couldn't. His emotions were too raw. Knowing how he was being set up, she still planned the glorious event for the head FBI agent? Not even considering how it'd make him feel?

He got into his truck and sped away. He caught sight of her in his rearview mirror, standing alone by the curb.

Alone.

She'd made her choice, and once more, it wasn't him.

The pain of that realization made him pull over to the side of the road and slam the steering wheel with the side of his fist.

She couldn't win for losing.

Ava turned and slipped into her car, heading back to the Renault Corporation. What was she supposed to do? Jocelyn was her friend and asked her to plan the wedding. She couldn't very well deny her friend simply because the groom was an FBI agent who came across as a hardnose. Did Max turn down real estate deals because it was someone she didn't like? Not hardly.

It was different. Yeah, she knew that, and she probably should've realized how it would hurt Max. But with everything else going on, she just hadn't considered it. Now she was stuck in the middle. Jocelyn or Max? It always came down to choosing with him. First her parents or him. Now her friend or him. Was God trying to tell her something?

Father God, I'm a mess. I need some serious wisdom.

She parked and headed into the building. A gust of a breeze kicked around the door as Ava marched across the foyer and slipped inside the elevator. At the top floor, she moved toward Dylan's office. Her office. Movement from inside captured her attention.

That Mildred! She was going to let the woman have it with both barrels.

Pushing open the door, she came up short.

Her mother's wheelchair was moved up to the desk, Mildred hovering just over her shoulder. Charla looked up at her entrance and frowned. "Well, well, well. How nice of you to join us, Ava."

"Mother." Ava gave a curt nod, then lifted her stare to the secretary. "That will be all, Mildred. I'll brief my mother."

A long moment followed where Mildred just stared at Charla. Finally, Charla nodded. "I'll buzz you when I'm ready to go back to my own office."

Mildred shut the door behind her.

"It's nice to see you in the office. I wa—"

Ice in Charla's stare stopped Ava. "What was Max Pershing doing in my company? In your brother's office?"

EIGHTEEN

No explanation was satisfactory.

Ava stammered and stuttered as her mother interrupted and ranted. After the weeks of shutting herself off from the world, Charla chose *now* to revert back to her old self?

When her tirade came to a halt, Charla glared. "What do you have to say for yourself, young lady?"

Taking in a deep breath, Ava silently prayed for strength and wisdom. And for God to give her the words to touch her mother's hardened heart. "I tried to tell you he was only helping me out. Only for a day."

"I'll not have that murdering rat step one foot inside my company again. Or around you, Ava Scarlett."

"I'm not seventeen years old anymore, Mother. You can't send me away to boarding school this time."

"Then I'll make sure you never enter the Renault Corporation again. Not even as a mail clerk."

Ava shrugged, not even angry. "I have my own business, in case you've forgotten. I only stepped in here to oversee things until you had your feet back under you, and from what I've seen today, you're back in true form. So I'm not needed."

"Then I'll disown you." Charla wagged a bony finger at Ava. "I'll write you out of my will."

"You don't get it, do you, Mother?" Ava shook her head. "I don't want your money—I never have."

"Then what do you want?"

Ava softened her tone as well as her expression. "The only thing I've ever wanted from you is your love and blessing."

"My blessing to see that man? Never. I won't allow it." Charla's voice rose even louder than before.

"I'm a grown woman, Mother. I'm quite capable of choosing my own dates."

"He murdered your brother. Don't you care?"

"Of course, I care." Ava moved to sit in the chair directly in front of her mother's wheelchair. "But I don't believe Max had anything to do with Dylan's murder. I believe with all my heart that he's being framed."

Charla harrumphed.

"I know you can't see it, but Max is a good man. He's kind and gentle, and if I decide to become involved with him, I'd like for you to accept that."

"Never."

Ava stood and sighed. "Then I guess there's nothing for us to talk about anymore. I won't have you threatening me with the Renault money. I don't need it, and if you're going to hold it over my head to manipulate my decisions, well, then I don't want it."

The anger in Charla's eyes was replaced by something else. Something Ava hadn't ever seen in her mother's eyes when she looked at her daughter. Something that looked like—respect.

"I love you, Mother. But I can't stand the threats. Not anymore. I just don't have it in me to keep fighting you."

Charla jutted out her chin in a defiant pose. "I'll have nothing to do with him or his vile family."

"That's your choice. I won't force Max on you, but you can't force me to not see him if I choose to do so."

"Well, that's *your* choice, I suppose."

It was the closest she'd ever come to winning an argument with her mother. Ava didn't know whether to be elated or depressed. But it was the proffered olive branch, and she was smart enough to take it.

"Fair enough." She pressed a kiss to her mother's temple.

Charla didn't jerk away from her touch. "Fine." Her voice was thick with emotion. Which emotion, Ava couldn't tell. "I'll see you at home tonight?"

"Of course, Mother." She left the office, a sense of connection to her mother calming her. Maybe they could build a relationship after all.

The late afternoon sun warmed the February air. In just a week or so, full Mardi Gras revelry would be in force. And Jocelyn's wedding. A wedding on Fat Tuesday…just like Jocelyn to want to be different.

Ava headed toward her office on Main Street. She needed to bring Cathy up to speed and take care of some tasks. Like making sure everything was set for the Halloway wedding. And for Jocelyn and Sam's.

Just thinking about the wedding reminded her of Max's reaction. Sure, she could understand him being upset, what with Sam being one of the investigators working the case, but she and Jocelyn were friends.

She pulled into the parking lot and sat for a moment before she went into the office. Maybe this was another sign from God that she and Max shouldn't be together. That he no longer shared her faith made it impossible for her to consider getting involved with him again, no matter how defiant she'd acted with her mother. She let out a sigh, got out of her car, walked to the building and pushed open the glass door.

Cathy sat at the front desk, busy typing on the computer and talking to the soon-to-be Mrs. Holloway. "Yes, ma'am. The musicians have already gotten set up in the ballroom. They'll rehearse tonight and be ready for your wedding in the morning."

What was it with people wanting a morning wedding these days?

Cathy made a gesture with her hand to indicate the woman was in a chatty mood.

Ava smiled, tossed her purse onto the couch adjacent to the desk and plopped down beside it, even going so far as to stretch out. Every part of her body wanted to be down for the count. She rested her head on the tapestry throw pillow and closed her eyes. The lack of sleep was catching up with her.

Now that she thought about it, Max's attitude toward her planning Jocelyn's wedding wasn't too different from her mother's in regards to Max. Could her life get anymore complicated?

Her cell phone rang. She grabbed it from her purse and flipped it open. "Hello."

"Ava? It's Clint. Clint Herald."

Oh, yeah, her life could get more convoluted. She suddenly lost her ability to speak.

"Hello? Ava?"

"Yes. I'm here. Sorry." Why was Clint calling her? How'd he get her phone number? Oh, yeah. She'd listed her cell phone in the phone book as a second number for I Dream of Weddings.

"Look, I wanted to call you. Sheriff Reed told me you were willing to have a DNA test..." He paused, as if waiting for her to jump in the conversation.

Her tongue remained in knots.

"I just wanted you to know that it's nothing personal. The reason I won't let a test be run on Sarah."

"Oh?" She finally found her voice, and she sounded like an imbecile.

"She's been through so much already. Even Ms. Gold doesn't think I should put her under any further stress."

"She'd never know what it was for. It's a swab in the mouth." Wow, she sounded like she was pleading. Begging. Maybe she was. Just to have a part of Dylan…the not knowing drove her up a wall.

"The thing is, until Leah comes back, I don't think I should do anything."

"Do you really think Leah will return?" Sad, but she had to admit, had Dylan just gone missing and not been found dead, she would cling to hope that he was alive somewhere. But after all this time and not returning for her daughter, the situation didn't look good for Leah.

"Yeah. I do. I feel it."

Could he be right and the FBI wrong? Sam sure thought Leah was dead. So did the sheriff. Then again, they both thought Max had killed Dylan. "I pray you're right. For Sarah's sake."

"Thank you. The prayers are truly appreciated." Another pause. "Well, I just wanted to let you know my refusal wasn't personal."

"I appreciate that." She closed the phone and stared at Cathy, still on the phone, without really seeing her.

Was Leah Farley still alive? If so, where was she? Hadn't there been talk right after she disappeared that she murdered her husband and ran off? And didn't someone say Leah and Angelina had argued just before then? Obviously there was a connection between Leah and Dylan. Could Leah be alive and picking off her enemies in Loomis, one by one?

"Maximilion Pershing, you're under arrest for the murder of Dylan Renault." Sam Pierce barged into the office, Sheriff Reed on his heels. "Please stand and place your hands behind your head."

Patsy stood in the doorway, tears in her eyes.

Blood rushing to his head and pulse pounding in his ears, Max stood and put his hands on the back of his head. "Pats, call Lyle Tanner for me. Tell him I've been arrested."

"You have the right to remain silent. Anything you say can and will be used against you in a court of law. You have the right…"

Max couldn't register the rest of what Sam said. The thumping of his heart drowned out everything when the cold metal of handcuffs wrapped around his wrist. His right hand-cuffed arm was brought down behind his back. His left followed, to be put in the other wrist bracelet. Fear lanced through his gut.

He stumbled as Sam led him from his office to the sheriff's cruiser. The sun beat down on him, but that heat wasn't what slicked Max's palms with sweat. The air held a coppery odor. Stale. The stench of his own fear.

Sam held his hand over Max's head and pushed to help him into the automobile. The stench of stale liquor was stronger. Or maybe Max's senses were in overdrive.

Being arrested for a murder he didn't commit. Never, in his wildest nightmares, could he have imagined this would happen.

They drove diagonally across the street and led him into the sheriff's station. He was fingerprinted, had a picture taken while holding a little sign and then put in the interrogation room. Alone. But not for long.

Sam waltzed in as if he owned the place. "Wanna tell me again how you're innocent?"

"I am."

"Then how are the tire tracks taken at the scene an exact match to the tires on your car?" Sam nodded. "That's right. The results from the castings are back. Ninety-nine percent of those tracks were made by your car."

Now he knew for sure. He *was* being framed!

"I wasn't there. Someone's setting me up."

"Yeah. Sure. Right. Who?" Sam sat on the edge of the table and towered over him.

"I don't know."

"You didn't report your car stolen."

"I didn't know it'd been driven."

"Who else has keys to your car?"

Max pinched his lips together. Only one other person had the keys to his car. On the key ring with the key to his condo.

His mother.

No, she wouldn't—well, would she? He'd have said no just a couple of days ago, but now, after learning what she'd done to Ava…he wasn't so sure. No, she wouldn't do this to him. Why would she?

"Who else has a key?"

"I'd like my lawyer."

Sam stood, shaking his head. "Of course you would." He stormed from the room, slamming the door in his wake.

Max rested his head in his hands. He was innocent. Arrested for a murder he didn't commit. By a man whose wedding was being planned by the woman Max loved.

He'd never felt so alone in his life.

Nothing made sense. He didn't understand. This was crazy.

Trust in the Lord with all your heart, and lean not on your own understanding.

Trust in God, through this?

A cloak of peace shrouded him.

Trust in the Lord with all your heart.

Could he trust God? Could he go back to leaning on Him at all times, but especially during trying times? But it didn't make sense.

Lean not on your own understanding. Trust in the Lord with all your heart.

Tears rose to his eyes, threatening to escape. All this time, he'd been trying to do things himself, solve all his own problems. Well, this was one he couldn't solve himself. There was no way out but by divine intervention.

Trust in the Lord with all your heart, and lean not on your own understanding.

Trembling, Max bowed his head and prayed to the God he'd resisted for more than ten years.

NINETEEN

Could the day have been any worse?

After finishing up at I Dream of Weddings, Ava slipped behind the wheel of her car. The sun kissed the horizon, shooting streaks of orange across the darkening sky. It'd been a long, horrible day. A very hot, very full bubble bath sounded like just the ticket to ease her stress. Followed by dropping into her bed and pulling the covers over her head. Tomorrow had to be a better day.

She backed out of the parking lot, steering toward home. She yawned, sleepiness creeping over her. Wouldn't do to fall asleep at the wheel at six o'clock. With the press of a button, the stereo blasted through the speakers. The local eighties station filled the car with a song she and Max had danced to at one of their high school homecomings. Great, just great.

Ava reached to turn the dial just as the song ended. She hesitated as the deejay came across the airwaves.

Now for this late-breaking story…Max Pershing, Loomis land developer and real estate mogul, has been arrested for the murder of business rival Dylan Renault. Mr. Pershing was taken into custody by

St. Tammany parish Sheriff Bradford Reed and FBI agent Sam Pierce. No statement has been made by either branch of law enforcement at this time regarding what led to the arrest of Pershing. Stay tuned for details as soon as they're released. This is Emily Miller, your drive-at-five host for KBAD.

Ava slammed on the brakes, and the car shimmied to the shoulder. Max…arrested? This couldn't be happening.

Her breathing came in gasps and spurts. If she didn't know better, she'd swear she was having an asthma attack. But she did know better, and that's what sent fearful adrenaline racing through her.

What had the police found in Max's car? They had to have found something convicting enough to have arrested him. This wasn't some threat. This was real.

She needed to know what was going on. Deserved to know. This was her brother's murder case. And the arrest of the man she'd never fallen out of love with.

Wait a minute…did she still love Max? Despite everything? No, she couldn't. There was too much painful history. Too much between them.

He was a suspect in her brother's murder.

He was framed.

He'd hurt her.

She'd hurt him.

He wasn't a Christian anymore.

That one stopped her arguments. She had no clue how she felt. Right now, all she could do was pray for him.

She shouldn't have asked herself the question if her day could be any worse. It'd taken a nosedive into the Worst Day Hall of Fame.

Yes, all she could do right now was pray. For Max. For the truth. For justice.

And ignore the little voice whispering in her ear that maybe she'd been wrong about Max.

Peace filled him.

It didn't matter what the FBI and the sheriff said, Max knew he was innocent. Beyond that, it didn't matter. He was back in harmony with God. Wasn't that all that counted?

Within moments, the door swished open and Lyle Tanner entered. The guard shut the door, leaving Max alone with his attorney. "Max."

"Lyle."

The lawyer pulled out the metal chair across the table from Max. It scraped across the grimy floor, sending goose bumps scattering over Max's back. "Okay, here's what they've got." He set a legal pad on the table and scanned his own handwriting. "Your medallion in Mr. Renault's pocket. An eyewitness that puts your car at the scene of the crime. And they've matched the casts from tire tracks made at the scene to the tires on your car. Compound all this with the ongoing family feud between the Pershings and Renaults, your past relationship with Ava Renault, and you have yourself as a prime murder suspect."

Well, spelled out like that, it was easy to see why they'd arrested him.

"But I didn't kill him."

Lyle glanced over his notes again. "When you met with Dylan the week before his murder, did you take your car? That could explain the matching tire tracks."

Thinking carefully, tapping into every ounce of his memory, Max slowly shook his head. "I took my truck."

"These tests are pretty conclusive, Max. Add in the eyewitness who places your car there, and any jury in America is going to believe you were at the murder scene."

How had he gotten into this situation? Nothing made sense.

"I didn't drive my car there. I can't explain this except to say I'm being set up."

The lawyer made a grumbling sound under his breath and flipped the page on his notebook. "Okay. Then let's see who could be setting you up. The person had to have access to the medallion. And your car. Give me some names of people with that kind of access to your property."

"Well, Ava and I already figured out that just about anyone could have gotten the necklace."

Pen poised over paper, Lyle stared at him. "Ava? As in Ava Renault?"

Max swallowed. "Yes. She believes I'm being set up, too."

"Whoa. Back up a minute. You and Ava have discussed the case?"

"Yes."

"Why on earth would you do that?" Lyle shuddered. "This is her brother's murder, Max. She can't be objective."

"Ava's not like that. She only wants the truth."

"Uh-huh." He scribbled on the paper. "So why does she believe you're being framed?"

"Because on the sheriff's inventory report of what was found on Dylan's body, the medallion was marked as being in his left front pocket. Dylan was right-handed and never put anything in his left pocket."

Lyle wrote faster. "Good. We didn't have access to that information."

"And then there's the matter of the hairs."

"Hairs?"

Max explained about the matching red hairs found on Earl Farley and Dylan, and the results that they came from a wig.

"I can't believe I wasn't provided this information."

"Maybe because they haven't found a red wig in my possession to link me to all the murders."

"This is good. The hair obviously links Dylan and Earl's murders, but you weren't even a suspect in Earl's death. You weren't in a family feud with Earl Farley, were you?" Lyle delivered the last question as a punch line.

"Well, actually…" His lawyer so wasn't going to like this connection.

"What?"

"In December, at the Christmas tree lighting ceremony in Loomis Park, Bartholomew Hansen and Earl got into an altercation. I helped break it up, and Earl got a bit mad at me."

"What, exactly, is a bit mad?"

"He yelled at me, cussed me out, told me to mind my business or I'd be sorry."

"What'd you say in response?"

Max shrugged. "I think I said something like if he didn't straighten up, he'd be the one who was sorry."

Lyle shook his head. "Is it too much to hope that no one else heard this exchange?"

"I know Bartholomew heard it. And others were standing around because when they went to exchanging blows, a crowd gathered."

"Great. This doesn't look so good for you, Max. They can tie you to Dylan's murder very easily, unless we can figure out how to cast reasonable doubt in the jury's mind, and now this will link you to Earl. The hair found on both will just be a further connection."

The strong sense of being overwhelmed and the situation being hopeless closed Max's eyes. *God, I know You and I just got back on speaking terms and all, but I sure could use some help down here. Pretty quick.*

"Help me out, Max. Think. The most damning evidence is your car. Besides you, who else has keys to the car? Or have you lost a key in recent months?"

"I haven't lost a key." And the only person who had a set of all his keys was his mother. But Max wasn't ready to discuss that with anyone. Not even his lawyer. Maybe she'd loaned his car to someone and failed to tell him. He couldn't just give her up without knowing the details. He knew all too well how the facts could be twisted and turned to make someone innocent look guilty.

His mother couldn't be involved in Dylan Renault's murder. No way, no how. She just didn't have it in her.

Of course he never thought she'd have it in her to lie to Ava's face and destroy their relationship, either.

She couldn't stay away.

No longer tired, Ava had driven around Loomis for a couple of hours. She didn't want to go home and face her mother, who by now surely had heard that Max had been arrested for Dylan's murder. She just didn't have it in her to fight her mother right now. Not when she knew Max was innocent.

And she knew she still loved him, even if they couldn't be together.

It was time for answers. Past time, actually.

Dylan was her brother, so she should be kept abreast of the investigation. She had every right to know what was going on.

At least, that's what she told herself as she headed to the sheriff's station. She ignored the hiccupping of her heart at the thought that Max had been arrested. For a crime she knew deep inside he didn't commit.

She parked and walked across the lot. The last vestiges of daylight disappeared, and night stole over Loomis. Tree frogs and crickets sang, welcoming the eerie darkness. A nippiness settled in the air. Ava felt the chill deep into her bones. She quickened her pace.

Without a clue as to what she would say, Ava opened the door to the sheriff's station. A wave of stale warmth breezed against her face. Stagnant air, reeking of old coffee and too many people confined in a small space, nearly made her gag. Not that anyone noticed.

The place hopped with activity. Phones rang, people moved about at a fast pace, printers hummed. A hub of noise kept getting louder and louder. Two local television crews hovered in the entry alongside Ava, a reporter knocking on the counter and asking to see someone about the arrest of Max Pershing.

She shouldn't be here. It'd been a mistake to come. But she had no choice. She had to see Max. Had to let him know she believed in his innocence. Ava shifted to keep her back to the news crews. The last thing she needed was to be caught up on a newscast.

Sam Pierce strode from the back of the station, caught sight of the newspeople and started to turn back around. Then, his gaze locked onto Ava's. He moved quickly to escort her behind the counter, much to the chagrin of the reporter, until she realized who the FBI agent had retrieved.

"Hey, Ava Renault. Are you here to see Max Pershing pay for murdering your brother?"

"Don't answer them. Don't even look at them," Sam whispered in her ear as he led her down the hall to an empty office.

They passed a deputy on the way. Sam pointed at the man. "There are television crews up front. Get them out of here. Now."

He led her into the office and shut the door. Turning to face her, he scowled. "What were you thinking coming down here? You shouldn't be here. It's a circus, and your presence only feeds all the gossip."

"I had to come." She grabbed his wrist. "Sam, Max is innocent. Someone's framing him."

He shook his head. "The evidence points directly to him."

"Because someone wants it to."

"Sorry. I'm not buying it."

"Please, listen."

He sighed.

"What if it was Jocelyn accused of something she didn't do? Wouldn't you want someone to hear her out?"

"What makes you think he's being set up?" His tone reflected he was merely humoring her, but at least he listened.

"That medallion."

"What about it?"

"It was found in Dylan's left front pants pocket. Dylan was right-handed."

Sam shrugged. "Semantics."

"No." She almost yelled but was beyond caring. "Listen to me. Someone is setting Max up. I know it."

He stared at her with such pity.

"Sam, I'm right. Look, this is my brother's murder we're talking about—I want to see justice served so badly. But not so badly that I'll settle just for the case to be closed. I want the truth."

"And you don't think Max is guilty? C'mon, Ava. I know there's a history between you and all, but we got a perfect match from the tire tracks made at the scene to his car tires. How can you explain that?"

She couldn't.

"You aren't his lawyer, Ava." He touched her shoulder. "Look, I know this is hard and very emotional for you, but let us handle this. Max's lawyer is here and if there's a mistake, he'll be sure to point it out to us." He let his hand fall. "Go home. Get some rest. You can call me tomorrow if you need to talk."

What else could she do? If Max's lawyer was here, she couldn't see him. She'd told Sam what she thought. There was nothing left for her to do but go home, as instructed.

She let out a sigh. "Okay."

"Let me take you out the back way and see you safely to your car. Those reporters can be vultures sometimes."

Oh, how well she knew that. They'd hounded Dylan relentlessly when he'd been questioned about Angelina's murder.

They ducked out the back door. No sign of any reporters.

A stillness hung in the air like a foreboding of evil. But evil had already descended upon Loomis, and it looked like it planned to stay awhile.

At her car, Ava smiled. "Thanks, Sam."

"No worries." He turned and walked back to the door.

A car screeched into the lot, making him spin around and freeze.

Lenore Pershing slammed her car into Park in the middle of lot, not even bothering to park in a space. She focused on Ava. "This is all your fault. All yours."

TWENTY

Shock held her tongue still. Ava could only stare at Lenore Pershing with wide-eyed wonder. The woman had lost her mind.

And she looked the part—hair flying out from her head, smeared makeup down her face and tattered sweatpants and T-shirt. She looked like an escapee from a mental institution. Not at all the image she'd worked for years to perfect.

She pointed a finger at Ava as she advanced. "This is all your fault. You turned on my boy."

"What? I haven't turned on Max. I never did. You're the liar."

Lenore drew closer, waving her hand in front of her. The security lights reflected off something in her hand.

Ava leaned against her car. The cold from the metal seeped through her light sweater. Had the woman gone totally nuts and brought a gun?

Dear Lord, what's going on?

"You told the police that medallion was Max's. They would've never known had you not turned on him."

"Lenore, I was shocked to see it in Dylan's belongings. The deputy was standing there when I found it." She caught sight of Sam in her peripheral vision. He stepped slowly from the doorstep, creeping across the parking lot.

"You were just supposed to stay away from him, not turn him in to the police. And you claimed to have loved him? I love him. I'd do anything to protect him. Especially from the likes of you." Max's mother stood not ten feet in front of Ava, her face contorted into rage and her arms shaking.

"I did love him. I still do."

Lenore's eyes widened and she huffed. "You can't have him. You couldn't years ago, and I won't let you now." She flailed her hands.

Ava squinted and made out what Lenore held in her hand. She recognized the shimmering gold.

Anger overtook her fear. "Is that a gold chain in your hand? The chain that the medallion was on?"

Sam froze from his position behind Lenore. He looked to Ava. No way would she let this woman get away with what she suspected Lenore had done. She gave Sam the slightest shake of her head.

"I'll not let you break his heart again. You're no better than your mother. You'd ruin my son."

Fighting to regulate her breathing, Ava took a step forward. "You set up your own son? Why?"

"I never meant for the police to figure it out. Bradford and his flunkies never would have. You weren't supposed to go running to them and tattling that the necklace was Max's. It was supposed to be just enough to keep you out of his life."

Never in her life had Ava wanted to hit someone so badly. But Sam motioned to her from behind Lenore, wanting her to keep the woman talking. Confessing.

"How'd you do it? I know you had access to the necklace and his car, but why'd you kill my brother?" She forced herself to remain calm.

"I didn't kill your brother, you stupid girl. I just seized the opportunity when it presented itself."

"How's that?"

"I was getting into the car when I noticed that drunk using the pay phone. What drunk makes calls?"

"Chuck? Chuck Peters?"

"Is there any other drunk?" Lenore shook her head and shifted her weight. "I heard him reporting Dylan had been shot and was lying in the grass by that stupid water fountain behind Renault Hall. He hung up, but I could tell from his reaction that the police hadn't taken him seriously."

"So what did you do?"

"Why, I rushed right over there, of course. I had to see if it was true. My goodness, do you know how long I've waited for that brother of yours to hang himself with the things he did? Flaunting around town, breaking girls' hearts. True Renault form. The apple doesn't fall far from the tree, does it?"

Ava bit her tongue so hard that she tasted the metallic tang of blood.

"Sure enough, the drunk was right. And I knew I'd been given a perfect opportunity to keep you out of Max's life forever."

"So you ignored my dying brother and planted the medallion?"

Lenore smiled the smile of a person gone off the deep end. "That was brilliant. I raced back to the car to find something of Max's I could leave there. Something that you would know belonged to Max but the police wouldn't. Driving his car that day, finding that stupid medallion he's worn every single day for years…well, I just know it was divine intervention."

"My brother was alive when you were there. Why didn't you call for help?"

Lenore snorted. "As if. He was mumbling nonsense—sorry to Leah, and little Sarah, and everything was all his fault. Of course, we already know that."

"If you didn't kill him, you had to have seen who did."

Sam shook his head vehemently.

"I saw no one but that playboy who'd finally gotten what he deserved."

"You could've saved him." Anger mixed with remorse, and Ava advanced toward the older woman. "You could've saved my brother and you let him die. You set up your own son for selfish reasons. What kind of person are you?"

Sam moved between the women and grabbed the chain from Lenore's hand. He handed it to Ava as he reached for the handcuffs on his belt. "Lenore Pershing, you're under arrest for interfering in an FBI investigation and planting false evidence at the scene of a murder. You have the right to remain silent. Everything you say can and will be held against you in a court of law."

Lenore glared at Ava. "This doesn't matter. Max has seen you for what you are—nothing but trouble."

Sam ignored her words and continued to read her the Miranda rights until done. "Do you understand your rights that I've read to you?"

"I'll be out in no time. Bradford won't let me see a day inside a jail cell. You can't do anything to me."

Smiling, Sam grabbed her by the arm and led her toward the station. "You think so, huh? Well, I've got news for you, lady. The FBI outranks a parish sheriff any day of the week." He halted and held out a hand toward Ava. "I'll need that chain as evidence."

Ava laid it in his palm. "What about Max?"

Sam cocked his head. "Well, since we have a confession of all the evidence that links him to your brother's murder, we'll have to dismiss all charges and let him go."

Tears burned the back of Ava's eyes. "Thank you," she whispered to Sam, then lifted her eyes to heaven and repeated the words, "Thank You."

* * *

"You're not giving me much to go on, Max." Lyle Tanner slipped his notepad into his briefcase. "If you're holding out on me, now's the time to come clean. I'm on your side, trying to help you."

Before Max could respond, a ruckus sounded from the hall.

"I want to see Bradford right now." There was no mistaking his mother's scream.

She'd heard about his arrest on the news and had come to get him out. She might have many faults, but not standing by her son wasn't one of them.

Lyle looked at Max. "Is that your mother?"

"Yeah. Probably here to raise all kinds of get-out for me having been arrested. She and the sheriff have an, uh, friendship of sorts."

Lyle pushed to his feet. "Stay here. Let me go see what's going on. She shouldn't have been allowed back here."

Max closed his eyes as the lawyer left. If his mother had heard about his arrest, then it stood to reason Ava had as well.

Ava.

Their past was so checkered, so woven with pain and lies. Could they ever move past that? He prayed so. He'd never stopped loving her, never stopped wanting a future with her. And once he figured out how to clear himself of this horrible mess, he'd tell her just that. No more wasting time.

"You're free to go." Lyle stood in the doorway with Agent Pierce just behind him.

"What?" Confusion filled Max.

"I'm sorry, Max. It seems your mother set you up." Lyle pushed his glasses up the bridge of his nose. "She told the whole story to Ava, and Agent Pierce here overheard the whole thing. She had the chain for the medallion in her hand."

"I don't understand."

Sam moved around the lawyer. "We're sorry for the inconvenience, Mr. Pershing. Why don't you allow Mr. Tanner to take you out the back door to miss the media circus out front? I think you'll find someone waiting out there who can fill you in on all the details."

He stood on wobbly legs and numbly followed his lawyer down the hall. He could still make out his mother's rants from behind a closed door somewhere. "Lyle, I'm confused."

"I can understand that. Let's just get out of here and I'll explain everything to you."

Max halted. "My mother. I can't leave her here."

Lyle took his arm and guided him to the back door. "Not now, Max. You need to hear some things first. You're in shock. Just come with me."

He stumbled out the door. Security lights flooded the steps, nearly blinding him. He could make out a figure in the parking lot. Descending the steps, the figure came into focus.

Ava. With her arms open wide to him.

He rushed forward and fell into her embrace. She held him tight, murmuring against his neck. Chills washed over him. He *knew* this was where he belonged. But why was she here? How did she know what was going on?

Stepping back, he looked into her eyes. "Mind telling me what the score is, Renault?" He used the old line they'd ask one another during football games.

She smiled. "Let's go somewhere we can talk. There's a lot you need to know. A lot you'll need time to process."

He glanced at his lawyer.

Lyle nodded. "Go with the lady, Max. I'll call you tomorrow and answer any questions you have."

"Hop in." Ava motioned to her car. "We'll drive out to the pier and talk."

How perfect. The first place he'd told her he loved her. And now the place he'd tell her he'd always love her.

Dear God, thank You. Thank You, thank You, thank You.

Somehow, he knew God had to be smiling down on them.

TWENTY-ONE

The pain in Max's beautiful eyes made her heart ache.

"I just can't believe my mother would go to such lengths."

The pier was deserted, except for the frogs croaking under the weathered boards. The temperature had dropped with the setting sun. An intermittent breeze flew off the bayou. Ava smiled despite the chill.

She held his hand, squeezing for reassurance. "I know. But, Max, you wouldn't have even recognized the look in her eyes. It was scary. Like she'd gone over the edge." She shivered, recalling the coldness in Lenore's orbs that matched her tone. "She scared me."

He rubbed his thumb over her knuckles. "I'm sorry."

"Don't be. She hurt you most of all. And that made me so mad."

"It makes me mad, too."

"You're going to be okay, Max. Everything will be all right. I know it's hard right now, I can't even imagine, but I have to believe everything's fine now."

"Ava, there's so much I need to say to you, but right now, my mind's just racing. I can't even think clearly."

She hurt for him. She couldn't imagine how he felt. Sure, Charla was a control freak and overbearing, but she'd never stoop so low as to frame her only son for a murder he didn't commit. Ava couldn't imagine what had to have gone through Lenore's mind.

"I understand. I'm just so sorry you're having to go through this."

"It'll all come out in the wash. God will give me strength to get through it."

Ava's heart stalled. Did he just say he'd lean on God? "Uh, Max, I thought you'd washed your hands of God."

He smiled, and tears glimmered in his eyes. "I thought I had, too, but you know what? When I was arrested and sat alone in that holding room, feeling like there was nothing I could do, nowhere I could go, lonelier than I've ever felt in my entire life, a certain Scripture ran through my head. The same Scripture someone quoted to me recently, and you prayed for us before we ate. That Scripture brought me to my knees, so to speak."

Ava couldn't find the words to express the celebration of her heart.

"So right then, in the middle of the sheriff's station, I asked God to forgive me and rededicated my life back to Him."

"Oh, Max." She ran a hand down the side of his face, letting it linger along his strong jaw. *Thank You, Jesus!*

His eyes clouded, a sign she recognized. Her heart pounded in response.

Ever so slowly, he leaned forward. He pressed his lips to hers. Gently, softly, like little feathery touches. A kiss that shook her to her toes.

Blood rushed to her head. She wound her arms around his neck, her fingers splaying through the back of his hair.

His arms enveloped her, pulling her close to his chest. So close she could feel the pounding of his heart. Her heartbeat raced to match his.

He deepened the kiss and she could feel the love simmering between them. A love that had been denied for entirely too long. Too many lies, too many years, too many wasted moments. The kiss held the promise of the future.

Pulling back, Max kept his gaze locked on hers. He ran a light finger down the side of her face. Goose bumps pimpled her arms. The hairs on the back of her neck stood at attention. She found it hard to breathe.

"Ava." Just her name. It sent spirals of butterflies loose in her stomach.

He bent his head and grazed his lips over hers. Before she registered they were on hers, they were gone. Nothing but a whisper of a kiss.

But enough that she knew she couldn't stand right now if her life depended upon it.

He wanted to tell her that he loved her. Needed to tell her. But now was not the time, or the place. He wanted it to be special. Something they'd remember forever, and he hoped they'd share the story with their children and grandchildren someday.

Standing, he helped Ava to her feet. "Come on, drive me home. I need to process everything that's happened."

Disappointment flashed across her face, and he was sorely tempted to draw her into his arms and never let her go. But he didn't want to rush into anything. And he didn't want to do anything without praying about it first.

He interlaced his fingers with hers and together, they walked down the isolated pier. No words were necessary.

She drove him to the condo in silence. Not strained, but very comfortable. The entire ride, he prayed. For guidance. For wisdom.

He opened the car door when she parked. "I'll call you tomorrow."

"You'd better." She smiled.

How simply they'd fallen into their old nighttime routine.

He leaned over and planted a kiss on her temple. The spicy perfume she wore entangled in his senses. He'd better get out of here and fast. With a quick wink, he slipped out and headed into his home.

Dark and quiet, the condo seemed to be holding its breath. For what, he hadn't a clue. He needed a shower to wash off the stench of the sheriff's station. And food. A lot of food. But he needed to do something else first. Something much more important.

God, help me forgive my mother. I know I should, but it's hard right now. But if You can forgive me for being such a stupid idiot all these past years, I know You can help me forgive her. And, God, I'd like to know Your will in regards to Ava. I love her so much, and I think she loves me too. But I don't want to be out of Your will. If You could just give me a sign …

An hour and shower later found him making stir-fry. The last time he'd made the dish, his mother had been there, giving him grief over Ava.

Had his mother suffered a nervous breakdown? There was no other explanation. He should call someone to go see her.

Goodness! He hadn't even asked Lyle to represent her.

Despite everything she'd done, she was still his mother. Grabbing the phone, he dialed Lyle's number while glancing at the clock. It wasn't ten yet, so maybe he wouldn't be disturbing him.

"Hello, Max."

Caller ID was a wonderful thing sometimes. "Hey, Lyle. I have a favor to ask."

"What's that?"

"Can you go to the sheriff's station and find out what's going on with my mother?"

"Are you sure?"

He hadn't missed the hesitation in Lyle's voice. "She's going to need a lawyer. You're the only one I know who handles criminal issues. And I trust you."

"I don't know, Max. I'm in the gray area of conflict of interest."

He hadn't even considered that. "I can't just not get her legal counsel, Lyle. She's my mother."

"In spite of everything?"

"She's still my mother."

Lyle sighed heavily over the connection. "Let me do some calling around. I have a colleague who lives in Covington who might be willing to take her case."

"Do you trust him?"

"He was my roommate in law school. Yes, I trust him."

"I'd really appreciate that. And having someone not from Loomis might not be a bad idea."

"I'll see what I can do. If he agrees, I doubt he'd come until morning."

Max thought of how horrible he'd felt inside the sheriff's station. He didn't want his mother going through that. Then again, the sheriff was sweet on her, so she'd probably be given the best accommodations possible. "I understand. Thanks, Lyle."

He ate his food in deep thought. How could his mother have done this to him? He'd have to keep praying for God's grace in helping him forgive her. Right now, he didn't want to. He wanted answers. Little by little, God would touch his heart, if he'd pray about it and but ask. He made the decision to keep praying. His heart might not be open to forgiveness just yet, but Max was determined to be obedient to God's directives.

The morning dawned bright and beautiful, the sun sneaking past the curtains to fill Ava's bedroom with sunlight and warmth. She stretched under the covers like a cat. Remembering Max's kisses from last night, she smiled.

Today was going to be a good day.

She showered and dressed, then entered the dining room with a bounce in her step.

And came to an immediate halt. Charla sat in her wheelchair at the end of the table, obviously waiting for her.

Ava misstepped, corrected, and took the seat closest to Charla. "Good morning, Mother. Isn't it a beautiful day?"

"I heard they arrested Max Pershing last evening for your brother's murder. I told you so."

"Actually, Max has been released. He *was* being framed, just like I told you." She reached for the cup of coffee Bea had just poured.

"By whom?" Her mother's brows were raised in that prissy way of hers.

No, Ava wouldn't lash out at her mother. Despite everything her mother did that drove her crazy, at least she wouldn't frame her children for murder.

"Lenore."

Charla spit coffee across the table. "Lenore Pershing framed her own son for Dylan's murder?"

Bea moved in an instant, wiping up the mess.

"She confessed." Ava lifted a casual shoulder, praying her mother wouldn't ask for more details.

"Well, well, well." Charla smiled, the first smile Ava had seen from her mother in days. "I always knew that woman was evil from the word go."

"Mother."

Charla's eyes hardened. "Did she kill my son?"

"She says no, and I think the police believe her."

"Bradford is an idiot and soft on her. Of course, he'd believe her."

"No. The FBI. She's been charged with framing Max and interfering in a federal investigation."

"So, who killed Dylan?"

"That's still unsolved." Which filled Ava with remorse and frustration.

"I see." Charla took a sip of the fresh cup Bea handed her.

No time like the present to lay her emotions out on the table, quite literally. She set her cup on the saucer. "Mother, I need to let you know I love Max Pershing, and if he's interested, I'm going to be dating him." She held up a hand to stop the tirade she saw flaming in Charla's expression. "This isn't up for discussion. I won't force you to accept him, but he will be a part of my life. If you can't handle that, I'll rent a place of my own and move out."

Her mother opened her mouth, then snapped it shut. A softness crept into the edges of her eyes. Just the edges, but it was a start. "I don't like it, Ava, and you know it. But you don't have to move out."

It was enough. For now.

She nodded and took a bite of the toast Bea slipped in front of her.

A knock on the front door interrupted the peaceful silence between mother and daughter. Moments later, Bosworth appeared with a vase of a dozen white roses. "Ms. Ava, where would you like these?"

Heart hopping, Ava jumped up and took the vase from the butler. She inhaled their heady scent, then reached for the card. Her fingers fumbled getting it out of the envelope.

God gave me a second chance. Will you?
All my love, Max

"Oh, my." Ava smelled the flowers again, her heart and spirit soaring.

"Where would you like the rest of them?" Bosworth asked.

"Rest of them?"

"Yes, ma'am. There are fifteen dozen in all, from what I understand."

"Fifteen dozen?!" Ava's hand flew to her mouth. A dozen for each year they were apart. Tears trailed down her cheeks. "I don't know, Bosworth."

The older man smiled. "I'll have them scattered across the house, madam."

"Thank you." Ava touched a petal.

"I wasn't aware the Pershings owned a florist."

Ava snapped her gaze to her mother's face. No malice lurked in the carefully made up lines. "Was that a joke, Mother?"

Charla pushed the button to back her chair from the table. "Don't be ridiculous, Ava Scarlett. Renaults don't make jokes."

Watching her mother roll out of the room, Ava smiled. This *was* a good day indeed.

Suddenly, the faint chords of "When a Man Loves a Woman" by Percy Sledge could be heard.

Their song.

She raced to the door, nearly knocking over Bosworth. The florist van moved, heading down the driveway.

Max sat on the hood of his truck, a portable CD player sitting beside him.

Her heart nearly stopped.

He slid to the ground and took two steps toward her.

She scampered down the stairs.

And into his waiting arms.

"Oh, Max."

"I love you, Ava. With all my heart."

Fresh tears spilled from her eyes. "And I love you. I always have."

Their kiss melded their hearts and spirits together.

This time for good.

EPILOGUE

Fat Tuesday delivered a magical day.

Ava accepted the hug from Jocelyn and Sam both. "It was perfect, girl. Thank you so much," Jocelyn gushed. As a bride, she was simply breathtaking. Her simple gown brought out her natural beauty—from the inside. Sam Pierce was a lucky man indeed.

Max stood at Ava's shoulder, looking proud. His close proximity kept Ava's heart fluttering all through the ceremony.

Sam offered his hand to Max. "I hope there are no hard feelings. I was just doing my job."

Max hesitated a moment, then shook Sam's hand. "But you have a totally different personality when you put the badge on."

Sam laughed. "I have to, man."

Ava smiled, her heart filled to bursting as she glanced around the park.

The outdoor wedding in the gazebo had been beautiful. She'd wondered—what with the invitations calling for guests to come in full Mardi Gras costume, but the event had been amazing.

Her own dress, green and purple satin, grazed the tips of her toes. She'd pulled her hair up into a French twist and decorated it with gold feathers. The look in Max's eyes when he came to pick her up made the extra time she took to get ready all worth it. And he looked dashing in his tuxedo.

Neither Charla nor Lenore was present, which made the gaiety even better. With Max and Ava a firm couple, the townspeople of Loomis didn't have to pick sides today. A blessing all around.

The park had been decked out in everything Mardi Gras. A zydeco band set up next to Pershing Provisions, which had irked Micheline Pershing. Max overruled her arguments. Even the day was warm and clear. Not a cloud in the sky.

The band started a slow song.

Max took her elbow. "Shall we, Ms. Renault?"

She laughed. "Most certainly, Mr. Pershing."

She stepped into his arms as if they'd never been apart. In her heart, they hadn't been. They moved together, gently swaying to the beat of the music.

What would her and Max's wedding be like? She'd plan the most perfect wedding ever. They deserved it.

Ava glanced around at the people crowding the dance floor. Sam and Jocelyn, looking like they stepped off the top of the wedding cake. Did she and Max glow like that?

Couples danced and laughed. A perfectly planned wedding. She needed to give Cathy a big bonus for all her help.

Off to the side, Clint Herald sat with Sarah on his knee. While he may not agree to a DNA test just yet, Ava wasn't going to give up hope. God was in the miracle business after all. Being in Max's arms right now was proof of that.

She let out a sigh. Happiness threatened to explode in her. Life was good.

Sheriff Bradford Reed, in his uniform, stepped onto the dance floor and tapped Sam on the shoulder. Ava was close enough to hear their exchange.

"I hate to interrupt you today."

"Then don't." Jocelyn glared at the local lawman.

"I don't have a choice."

"What is it?" Sam growled.

"A shoe that's been identified as belonging to Leah Farley has been found."

Jocelyn twisted to spy Clint and Sarah in the corner of the park. Sam took Jocelyn's hand and followed the sheriff off the dance floor.

Ava tugged Max behind them. No way was she going to miss this conversation.

"Where?" Sam asked.

"Out near the old pier. By an old house that's been boarded up. It was once a stop on the underground railroad. There's a door in the root cellar beneath it that opens into a narrow tunnel which leads to a room where escaped slaves once hid. We boarded up the entrance to the tunnel many years ago to keep kids out, but when we found the shoe near the back door of the house, we found that the boards covering the entrance to the tunnel have been pulled down and haphazardly replaced."

Sam hesitated, clearly being sucked back into the investigation but wanting to stay with Jocelyn.

She rose on tiptoe and planted a kiss on his cheek. "Go. This town deserves answers to what happened to our citizens."

Sam gave Jocelyn a quick kiss before leaving with the sheriff.

Ava put an arm around her friend. "An FBI agent…it's always going to be something, isn't it?"

"Yeah." Jocelyn glanced over to Clint and Sarah again. "But I meant what I said. Loomis needs to know the truth of what happened to Earl, Leah, Angelina and Dylan."

"I know." Ava dropped her arm from Jocelyn's shoulders and snuggled into Max. "We do need answers."

"I'm going to talk to Clint." Jocelyn headed across the park.

Max turned Ava to face him. "We might not have the answers to what happened to everyone yet, but God asks us to trust in Him, with all our hearts."

"I do."

"I know, and that's one of the many reasons I love you so much." He kissed her lips, then held her tight.

She did trust God with all her heart, but she sure hoped answers to what happened would be uncovered soon.

Very soon.

* * * * *

Dear Reader,

This has been a fun adventure for me—to work with five other amazing Love Inspired Suspense authors to produce this series. It's been a great honor to work with them and see this series all brought together. I've so enjoyed being a part of the group.

The characters in all of the books are so complex and diverse. It's been fun watching them work through their inner struggles and overcome.

Ava and Max's story reminds me of a modern-day *Romeo and Juliet*. Sharing their love amid a backdrop of mystery and suspense was both challenging and gratifying. Max being accused of a crime he didn't commit is a story line that's very close to my heart. Bad things sometimes happen to good people and we may never understand that—we just have to trust in God with all our hearts. I hope you've enjoyed learning more about the people from Loomis.

I love hearing from readers. Please visit me at www.robincaroll.com and drop me a line, or write to me at P.O. Box 242091, Little Rock, Arkansas 72223. Join my newsletter group and sign my guest book. I look forward to hearing from you.

Blessings,

Robin Caroll

QUESTIONS FOR DISCUSSION

1. Ava's mother ripped apart Ava and Max's young love. Have you ever had someone interfere with your relationships? How did you handle the situation?

2. Max felt as if God wasn't answering his prayers. Have you ever felt that way? How did you work through your disappointments?

3. Dylan didn't have a great reputation around town, which upset Ava. Have you ever had to live down a reputation or one of a relative? What is the best way to deal with the situation?

4. Max was accused of a crime he didn't commit. Have you ever been falsely accused of something? How did you overcome it?

5. Ava felt inferior around her overbearing mother. Have you ever felt that way? How did you reconcile your emotions?

6. Max's and Ava's mothers were domineering and interfering, sometimes to extremes. Have you ever had to deal with someone close to you with those character traits? How did you handle the relationship?

7. Ava felt as if she'd been pushed into a profession she hadn't really wanted to pursue. Have you ever been in a similar situation? What did you do?

8. Law enforcement doesn't always get it right. Have you

ever been convinced that law enforcement was wrong in a particular situation? How did you handle that in a Christian manner?

9. Ava had made mistakes in her past, acting out because she was hurt. Have you ever acted out? Explain.

10. Max and Ava had to learn to trust one another again in order to reclaim their love. How important is trust to you in your personal relationships?

11. Ava battled with herself about Max's possible involvement in her brother's death. Have you ever warred within yourself about another person? What happened?

12. Micheline Pershing showed great rudeness at Dylan's funeral. How have you dealt with rudeness in people?

13. Ava and Max were each raised to hate the other because of an old family feud. Has someone ever tried to persuade you not to like someone based on the past actions of others? How did you handle the situation?

14. Max returned to God when he felt all alone in the world. Have you ever felt like that? What did you do?

15. Ava loved Max and prayed for his salvation. How might you help someone you know is unsaved?

Turn the page for a sneak preview of the next book in the exciting WITHOUT A TRACE series.

COLD CASE MURDER by Shirlee McCoy goes on sale in March 2009.

Chapter One

Loomis, Louisiana
Early March

Even with the windows of her car rolled up, FBI agent Jodie Gilmore could smell the bayou. Heavy, moist air with a bite of decay to it. Not as bad as it got in the heat of the summer, but bad enough to make her nose wrinkle. Or maybe it was disgust that was doing that. There were plenty of places she'd imagined the FBI might send her, but back to Loomis wasn't one of them. Here she was, returning to the one place she'd been determined never to visit again.

She turned onto a narrow dirt driveway that wound uphill and away from the bayou, braking lightly as she neared a neglected farmhouse that stood in the center of an overgrown clearing near the swamp. Abandoned decades ago, it had been vacant for more years than Jodie had been alive. A tunnel dug beneath the house led to a room that had once served as a stop on the Underground Railroad. Later it had served other, less altruistic purposes—a storage place for moonshine during

Prohibition and a drug den for hippies in the sixties. Eventually the town council had voted to have the tunnel and the house boarded up.

What the missing woman, Leah Farley, had been doing there, Jodie didn't know. She planned to find out though. And quickly. The sooner she helped Sam Pierce solve the case, the sooner she could wipe the Loomis dirt off her feet and get back to her life.

Rain drizzled from the sky as Jodie climbed out of her car and started across the yard. Despite her misgivings about being back in Loomis, anticipation hummed through her. Working for the FBI had been her dream for as long as she could remember. Solving cases, putting bad guys behind bars was what she was meant to do. Even if she had to do it in Loomis.

"Agent Gilmore, glad you could make it to the party." A tall, dark-haired man she recognized stepped out onto the porch, and Jodie smiled a greeting as she made her way up dry-rotted porch stairs.

"It's good to be included, Agent Pierce."

"How about I call you Jodie and you call me Sam? It'll make things easier." He smiled, and Jodie could see why so many women in the New Orleans office had set their sights on the handsome agent. Recently, rumors had been circulating that he'd gotten engaged to a child psychologist in Loomis. True or not, it wasn't any of Jodie's concern. She didn't waste time on men and relationships. Not anymore.

"Whatever you say, Sam. Did you find anything in the house?"

"We did."

"Leah Farley?"

"No. And no evidence that she's been inside."

"So what did you find?" Curious, Jodie followed Sam into

the musty foyer, her mind racing with possibilities. Ransom note. Clothing. Forensic evidence. Any of those could help bring the case to a successful end.

"We found two bodies."

"*Two* bodies?" She glanced around the dust-covered foyer, half expecting to see the remains lying nearby.

"Skeletons, to be more accurate. They're in a hidden room down in the basement. They've been there for a while. Decades probably."

"Did they have identification?"

"Not that we could see, but the sheriff agreed not to let anyone touch the remains yet. I've got a man coming in from New Orleans to do that. A forensic anthropologist."

"When will he get here?"

"Shouldn't be long. I called him an hour ago."

"Do you mind if I take a look at the scene while we wait?" Now that she was in Loomis, Jodie wanted out of it. Waiting for someone to come along and help make that happen didn't work for her.

"Sure. It's this way."

Half-rotted boards creaked beneath her feet as Jodie followed Sam into the basement. The sound sent shivers along her spine, reminding her of all the stories she'd heard about the house when she was a kid, stories about spooks and haunts and things that went bump in the night. Jodie had always known them for what they were—a perfect way to keep kids from exploring a house that might not be structurally sound. Still, she had to admit the place was creepy, its shadowy corners concealing more than they revealed.

"Careful on these stairs, Jodie. Some of them are completely rotted through." Sam led her into a basement lit by electric torches and gestured to a hole in the far wall. "There's the tunnel. There were boards covering it, but it looked like they'd been taken down and replaced quickly. We've already got them tagged as evidence."

Several uniformed officers were standing in the room, none of them familiar to Jodie. She had to admit she was relieved. Eventually she'd have to face people from her past, but she'd rather it be later than sooner.

She crossed the room and surveyed the opening. Five feet high. Maybe three feet wide. "It would be a tight squeeze for someone carrying a body."

"But not so tight it would be impossible. Especially not if the body was being dragged. After so long, there isn't evidence to indicate that's what happened, but we can't say it didn't either. Hopefully Cahill will shed some light on things."

"Cahill?"

"The forensic anthropologist I told you about. He'll recreate the scene based on what he finds, then work to identify our victims. Come on in, but watch your head." He stooped down and walked into the tunnel.

Jodie borrowed a flashlight one of the officers offered and followed. "*Our* victims? Isn't the case a local matter?"

"It should be, but since we were in here following up on the Leah Farley case, the sheriff asked if we'd be willing to help with victim identification. I agreed."

"Who's the sheriff around here now?" Hopefully not the same one who'd been sheriff when Jodie was growing up.

"Bradford Reed."

Of course it was the same sheriff. Otherwise, things would have been a little too comfortable. "I remember him."

"Good. The Leah Farley case may be connected to the murders that have occurred in town. Getting along with the local PD is imperative."

Then you shouldn't have called me in to help.

Jodie didn't say what she was thinking. There was no way

she wanted to explain her teenage years. The subtle rebellions that had, more often than not, gotten her in trouble.

The scent of damp earth filled her nose, and cool, moist air settled on her skin as she stepped into a cavernous room. Her flashlight beam bobbed across a dirt floor littered with years of debris. Cloth. Plastic. A few old bottles. Near the far wall, a pile of rotted clothes lay amidst the other rubble. Even without getting closer, Jodie could make out the shapes of the bones beneath. Two skulls lay side by side in the dirt, smooth and dingy yellow.

She moved closer, doing her best to stay detached and un-affected as she surveyed the remains. Stale air, ripe with the remnants of something putrid and old, filled her lungs. She ignored it, crouching down to get a better look. A fleshless skull stared up at her, its empty eye sockets and grinning teeth a macabre reminder of the life that had once been. The other skull was facedown, a two-centimeter sliver of bone missing from its base. Closer to the top of the skull, the bone was cracked.

"It would take a lot of force to crack a skull like that." She spoke the thought out loud, wanting to pick the skull up and examine it more closely, but knowing she couldn't.

"A lot of force or a lot of rage."

"Any sign of the weapon?"

"Nothing. From the looks of the injury, we could be looking for anything. Baseball bat, butt of a gun, a club."

"Maybe something metal. A pipe?" Jodie responded by rote, her gaze riveted to a pile of hair that lay beside the skulls. It looked as if a rodent had made a nest there, creating it from faded cloth and long strands of fine hair. Blond hair, from the looks of it. Even time and dirt couldn't quite hide the fact. More tufts of it were visible beneath the facedown skull. These were even easier to identify. Long. Straight.

White-blond?

If so, they were the same color as Jodie's. The same color her mother's had been. She shuddered, leaning in a little closer, trying to see more of what remained.

"You're getting a little close to the remains, ma'am. Maybe you should back up before you disturb something." The words were gruff and loud, and Jodie whirled toward the speaker, her flashlight illuminating a tall, dark-haired man who stood beside Sam.

"I'm not in the habit of disturbing crime scenes."

"Good to know." He strode across the room, his movements as lithe and graceful as a jungle cat's, his gaze so intense Jodie was tempted to look away.

"I take it you're the forensic anthropologist." She stood, careful not to step any closer to the skeletons.

"Harrison Cahill." His eyes were oddly light in a craggy face, his lips turned down in a scowl.

"Jodie Gilmore."

"I take it you're the agent working with Sam? And a fairly new one, right?" He said it almost absently as he moved up beside Jodie, his gaze moving from her to the mound of cloth and bones.

"Does it matter?"

"I guess we'll find out." He met her eyes for a moment, then crouched down next to the skeletons, dismissing her with an abruptness that bordered on rude.

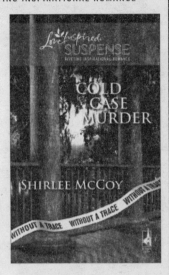

REQUEST YOUR FREE BOOKS!
2 FREE RIVETING INSPIRATIONAL NOVELS
PLUS 2 FREE MYSTERY GIFTS

YES! Please send me 2 FREE Love Inspired® Suspense novels and my 2 FREE mystery gifts (gifts are worth about $10). After receiving them, if I don't wish to receive any more books, I can return the shipping statement marked "cancel". If I don't cancel, I will receive 4 brand-new novels every month and be billed just $4.24 per book in the U.S. or $4.74 per book in Canada, plus 25¢ shipping and handling per book and applicable taxes, if any*. That's a savings of over 20% off the cover price! I understand that accepting the 2 free books and gifts places me under no obligation to buy anything. I can always return a shipment and cancel at any time. Even if I never buy another book, the two free books and gifts are mine to keep forever.

123 IDN ERXX   323 IDN ERXM

Name	(PLEASE PRINT)	
Address		Apt. #
City	State/Prov.	Zip/Postal Code

Signature (if under 18, a parent or guardian must sign)

Order online at www.LoveInspiredSuspense.com
Or mail to Steeple Hill Reader Service:
IN U.S.A.: P.O. Box 1867, Buffalo, NY 14240-1867
IN CANADA: P.O. Box 609, Fort Erie, Ontario L2A 5X3

Not valid to current subscribers of Love Inspired Suspense books.

Want to try two free books from another series?
Call 1-800-873-8635 or visit www.morefreebooks.com

* Terms and prices subject to change without notice. N.Y. residents add applicable sales tax. Canadian residents will be charged applicable provincial taxes and GST. Offer not valid in Quebec. This offer is limited to one order per household. All orders subject to approval. Credit or debit balances in a customer's account(s) may be offset by any other outstanding balance owed by or to the customer. Please allow 4 to 6 weeks for delivery. Offer available while quantities last.

Your Privacy: Steeple Hill Books is committed to protecting your privacy. Our Privacy Policy is available online at www.SteepleHill.com or upon request from the Reader Service. From time to time we make our lists of customers available to reputable third parties who may have a product or service of interest to you. If you would prefer we not share your name and address, please check here. ☐

Love Inspired
SUSPENSE

TITLES AVAILABLE NEXT MONTH
Available March 10, 2009

POISONED SECRETS by Margaret Daley
An anonymous tip brought Maggie Ridgeway to her birth
mother. Yet finding her led to more questions. Why did
her parents abandon her? What's triggering the *multiple*
burglaries in her new apartment? Can building owner
Kane McDowell protect her? And once he finds out
who she really is, will he still want to?

COLD CASE MURDER by Shirlee McCoy
Without a Trace
Loomis, Louisiana, holds no charms for Jodie Gilmore. Still,
the novice FBI agent has a job to do, investigating the local
missing person's case. But the job gets complicated when
handsome forensic anthropologist Harrison Cahill uncovers
a decades-old double homicide.

A SILENT TERROR by Lynette Eason
There was no motive for the murder—Marianna Santino's
roommate shouldn't have died. Then Detective
Ethan O'Hara realizes the deaf teacher was the *real*
target. Ethan learns all he can about Marianna. Soon, he's
willing to risk everything—even his heart—to keep her safe.

PERFECT TARGET by Stephanie Newton
The corpse in her path was the first warning. Next was a
break-in at Bayley Foster's home. She's certain that the
stalker who once tormented her has returned to toy with
her again. Her protective neighbor, police detective
Cruse Conyers, is determined to get answers—at any cost.

LISCNMBPA0209